01   11

A WREATH OF LORDS AND LADIES

By James Fraser

A WREATH OF
LORDS AND LADIES

c1

JAMES FRASER

PUBLISHED FOR THE CRIME CLUB BY
DOUBLEDAY & COMPANY, INC.
GARDEN CITY, NEW YORK
1975

All of the characters in this book
are fictitious, and any resemblance
to actual persons, living or dead,
is purely coincidental.

ISBN: 0-385-11074-X
Library of Congress Catalog Card Number 75–5261

for Blancoquiere

The whole village was silent, waiting. By unspoken agreement no one drove a car down the High Street but carried straight on down Nether Way making the detour by Five Ends. There was silence along Hall Way and along the avenue of elms that led to the Hall. It was dusk and pools of shadow lay beneath the trees, darker even than the sky above. There were no stars yet. The Hall ahead loomed large and dark, its only lights above the porticoed front door, the library, and the master bedroom on the first floor. The Reverend Thomas Dalgleish walked hurriedly but silently between the elms and up to the front door. He was wearing a black overcoat and carried a Bible and a Book of Common Prayer in his right hand. Bare-headed, his prematurely silver hair reflected the light above the door. As he arrived at the top of the five steps that led to the porch, the door opened to reveal Arthur Porter, wearing a black coat, a wing collar, a silver tie, and striped trousers. On his face was a grave and solemn look.

"He's still with us?" Thomas Dalgleish asked. Porter nodded without speaking, stood to one side to allow the vicar to pass, then silently closed the heavy iron-studded door. They stood for a moment in the dark hall.

"Her Ladyship wanted the lights switched off," Porter said by way of explanation. At that moment a door must have been opened on the first floor for a shaft of light shone from above and bathed the panelled entrance hall in a soft glow which revealed sombre dark wood, grey flagstones, stone archways, the portraits that stared down from the side of the solid stone staircase with its carved stone balustrade.

"Is that the vicar?" a voice asked, hard and piercing, a voice accustomed to commanding the long distances of the grounds or the hunting fields.

"Yes, my Lady," Porter replied.

"Bring him up, Porter," she said, as if the vicar were a delivery from some grocer's shop.

Porter beckoned with his hand and the vicar preceded him up the staircase.

Lord Bushden was lying on his bed, wearing a woollen maroon dressing gown with gold piping, a heavy tasselled cord, and the Bushden family insignia embroidered on its breast pocket. His unslippered feet projected beneath the robe, and he was wearing maroon silk pyjamas. The bed was unmade beneath him, as if he had flung back the covers when he got out and had not troubled to replace them when he lay down again. The room was filled with heavy mahogany furniture that had known the rub of countless generations. It was carpeted in thick Axminster, and the curtains, now undrawn, were of heavy brocade. The bed itself, enormous in size, had a heavy headboard carved by Grinling Gibbons and a low footboard to match.

Lord Bushden's face was the colour of old candles; his white stringy hair revealed his three score years and ten. His hands were crossed on one of the gold tassels of his robe, and his long bony fingers twitched impatiently. The vicar stood beside the bed. Lady Bushden went to the other side and tried ineffectually to smooth the bed over. Arthur Porter stood near the door. When Lord Bushden spoke his voice rumbled from his chest, his words blurred by his lack of teeth. The vicar bent forward. Lord Bushden's right eye opened. "Didn't you hear me, Vicar?" he asked petulantly. The vicar craned his head forward even farther.

"I didn't quite catch what you said, my Lord."

Lord Bushden's fingers twitched again impatiently "I've asked her and she won't do it," he said, his eye flicking towards Lady Bushden. "I've even asked Porter and the old scoundrel refused me. Perhaps you'd be good enough to do as I bid."

The effort his words were costing him was clear. Lady

Bushden looked at the vicar beseechingly, as if to say "Humour him by all means, but don't let him speak too much."

"What is it you want, my Lord?" the vicar asked.

The deterioration in Lord Bushden's condition was obvious. The vicar had stood too often beside the beds of the dying not to know the imminence of death.

Lord Bushden spoke again, his thin lips pursed, his face drawn with conscious effort. "Cain and Abel," he said slowly and painfully. "It was ever thus." Then his other eye opened, glittering brightly. He tried to move his hand to clasp the hand of the vicar but it was apparent he could not do so. The vicar reached out and held the hand of Lord Bushden.

"Fetch the police, there's a good man," his Lordship said. The focus went from his eyes. His features finally relaxed. His breathing stopped. Lady Bushden gave a long deep sigh, the vicar reached forward, closed Lord Bushden's eyelids, and opened the Book of Common Prayer.

A WREATH OF LORDS AND LADIES

CHAPTER ONE

Detective Superintendent Bill Aveyard stirred the cream sauce, lifted the spoon to his lips and tasted it. He reached to the shelf beside the gas stove, brought down a pepper mill and turned it twice over the cream sauce. Then he tasted again.

"I hope you don't mind eating early," he said to the girl sitting on the sofa on the other side of the screen which separated the sitting room of his flat from the kitchen.

The girl looked up from the book she had been reading. "Not at all," she said. "Is there anything I can do to help?"

Bill Aveyard shook his head. "It's all ready," he said, "and we have plenty of time before we need leave for the pictures." He poured the cream sauce into a jug which he placed on the tray. He took the mushrooms from under the grill and arranged them on the toast already waiting on the warmed plates. A quick check. Wine, not too cool, two glasses, mushrooms on toast with cream sauce, two of the linen napkins Irish Bill had brought back from Dublin for him after his release; everything in order. He carried the tray through and set it by the sofa. "We can eat here," he said. "It's not worth laying the table."

Her eyes were shining at him. "You can cook too," she said. "That smells delicious."

He reached over and nibbled beneath her ear. "And you smell delicious too," he said. A shiver ran down her back.

"We don't have to go to the pictures."

"You're a glutton," he said, smiling at her.

The telephone rang. "That'll be Jim Bruton," he said. "I asked him if he wanted to come to the pictures with us."

She pouted. "I thought we were going to be alone."

He had his hand on the receiver. "We will be," he said, "after the pictures." He picked up the telephone.

"Aveyard."

The voice at the other end of the telephone growled, low, deep and ominously familiar. "Since the police force is paying for the rental of your telephone as a necessary business expense, I think you might at least answer it with your rank, *Superintendent* Aveyard."

Bill Aveyard's heart, high in anticipation of the evening ahead, sank with the speed of an express lift into his boots. "Yes, Chief," he said.

"Right, Superintendent. I'll bet you were just about to have your supper."

"Yes, Chief."

"I bet there's a young lady sitting on your sofa."

"Yes, Chief."

"And I bet you were planning the sort of evening that would make the chief matron of a girls' prison blush. Don't bother to tell me you're off duty. Wilkins has a smash and grab, Peters is on leave, and Thomas has just reported sick with a broken ankle. As for me, I've just received Cuthbert's new seed catalogue, and I have my shoes off and my feet up."

"What is it, Chief, where and who?" Bill Aveyard was suddenly all copper. He knew that beneath the banter the chief would not have called him on duty unless it was something urgent and of great importance. He looked across at the girl. She made a face at him.

"Lord Bushden. Bushden Hall. Just died. Last words were spoken to the vicar. 'Fetch the police.' Message received five minutes ago via his butler, name of Porter, Arthur. Go find out why he wanted a copper, while he's still warm. The beat man, Jolly Rogers—remember?—is standing outside the bedroom door."

"Anything known, Chief?" Aveyard asked.

"Nothing criminal, but Lord B was worth millions and his son and heir, David Arthur of that ilk, is an idiot who ought to be in St. Crispin's."

Aveyard put down the telephone, looked across to the girl on the sofa. "I hope you have a good appetite," he said, "because I cooked an awful lot of mushrooms on toast."

CHAPTER TWO

Bushden Hall was rebuilt in the late thirteenth century after a fire had destroyed the demesne which occupied the site overlooking the banks of the river Nene. A comparatively small edifice as halls go, it contained only thirty rooms, of which the undoubted *pièce de résistance* was a galleried dining hall some sixty feet long and forty feet wide. The domed roof, over twenty-five feet high, contained a perfect example of fourteenth-century timbering. At the time of the Reformation the north wing was extended and stables and an Orangery of imposing proportions were added. Only the master builder however, Joseph Peckwith, a Catholic, knew that the construction concealed a space. Into that space Italian workmen, brought in by night, installed Priest Chambers whose entrance was unknown except to Peckwith, Isaiah Bushden, and the Italians who knew no English and were quickly taken home at the completion of their secret task.

Thomas Bushden, the descendant of Isaiah, who occupied the house during the time of the Guy Fawkes conspiracy, was a humanist and philosopher who cared nothing for adherence to any particular formal faith. When it became punitive to profess to a belief in Roman Catholicism, he became a Protestant. If the reigning monarch had been a Buddhist or had worshipped Islam then Thomas Bushden would have followed his credo without hesitation. Documents recently discovered in a cavity in a wall at Rushton have indicated that Thomas Bushden probably sheltered

Catesby and five of his fellow conspirators on their way to Ashby St. Ledgers after the failure of the Gunpowder Plot. He then provisioned and rehorsed them for their ill-fated final journey to Holbeach in Staffordshire, where Catesby and Percy standing and fighting back to back were both mortally wounded with one musket ball.

Very little had needed to be done to Bushden Hall in the intervening period except for a modernization of the water, light, and heating systems, the installation of a stainless kitchen and the repair and preservation of the famous timbered roof. The fortunes of the Bushden family were derived from land and foreign investment. The East India Company in particular had contributed enormously to the family wealth, worth many million pounds. Lord Bushden, who succeeded to the title and the estate in 1933, had managed his affairs throughout the years with impeccable dignity, courtesy, and discipline. During the last war he served as an officer with the Artillery and though he won no medals he conducted his battery with the same stringent attention to ethic as he had run his house and family.

Lord Bushden died a much respected man. Though he had been a stickler for tradition, his heart was benign. The village of Bushden had been part of the estate since time immemorial and he knew every occupant personally and by name. He remembered the birthday of every person in the village. A gift from his Lordship of twenty pounds, never more, never less, was the cherished dowry of every girl who married. The men received a five pound note. His contribution to every social and charitable occasion in the village, the Church fête, the Young Farmers' Social, the Annual Memorial Dance, was always twenty pounds.

These had been his formal and overt gifts, but in addition it was known, though never said, that Lord Bushden had an ear into which all troubles could be poured. Each evening he sat in his study to the right of the front door, which was always left ajar between the hours of six and seven o'clock.

A tap on the door of his study would elicit a deep, "Come in." He would put down the book he was reading, cross his hands, identify his visitor by name. "Well, James, what can I do for you?" Any person living in the village knew he could pour out his troubles and they would be heard with sympathetic understanding and answered with wisdom. More often than not the solution would be a piece of worldly advice. If money were required because of some folly or sudden misfortune then money would be forthcoming, taken in cash from the top right-hand drawer of Lord Bushden's desk. Invariably over the years the money, of which no record was kept, would be repaid. Such was the nature of the giving and such the gratitude of the recipient.

Lord Bushden married Emily, second daughter of Lord Cartwright, in 1939 on her twenty-first birthday. He was thirty-seven years old and a handsome artillery officer; it was a love match of idyllic proportions. In 1943 Emily, Lady Bushden, gave birth to a boy they named David Arthur. Two years later, another boy was born by Caesarian section and named Rupert Samuel. Emily was told after the birth that she could have no more children; she was disappointed her second child had not been a girl but she looked at the two sons she had produced and was content. It wasn't until David Arthur was ten years old that finally she accepted the diagnosis of the last of the many physicians she had consulted over the years, that the boy would never be any other than a comparative simpleton.

The chief cause of Lord Bushden's worry, however, was contained in the part of his title that dealt with the succession. When the title had been granted, it had been decreed in the Royal Letters Patent that the line of the succession should always be through the first-born son. However, the Letters Patent contained one unusual proviso. If, after succeeding to the title, the first-born failed to produce an heir himself, then on his death the title could not pass laterally to a brother.

However, if it should so happen that the first-born died before he succeeded to the title, then the title would pass, on the death of the father, to the next son in line. If David Arthur had died in childhood, Rupert Samuel would be in line for succession. If David Arthur's mental capacities were in doubt, it would be unlikely that eventually he'd marry and produce an heir. He was, however, physically healthy, and it seemed equally unlikely that he would die before his father. Either way, Rupert Samuel had little hope of ever becoming Lord Bushden, and on David Arthur's eventual death the title would die out.

All this had distressed Lord Bushden for several years but gradually, being a religious man, he was able to accept it as the Will of God, part of the Divine Pattern by which all life is ruled. As the years passed he became more and more fond of the boy who one day would take his place and slowly, with infinite patience, he tried to instil into him the significance, the importance, that would attach itself to being Lord Bushden, of Bushden.

It almost began to seem as if the mental ability that should have been David Arthur's portion had been vested in the second son, Rupert Samuel, who had twice the intelligence of a boy his age. He did brilliantly at Eton, took a double first at Oxford and graduated *summa cum laude* from the Business School at Harvard. In one year he completed the two-year course in estate management at London University and returned home to take up the reins of the family estate. His father, by now sixty-nine, had been told by the Harley Street specialist that he was suffering from a malignant tumour of the brain, and handed over to Rupert Samuel with relief. Things went well for several months and the estate profits leaped under Rupert Samuel's management.

One evening Lord Bushden was walking in the village about six o'clock. He'd erected a stand of poplars south of the village a couple of years back and had had a whim after tea to see how they were doing. The poplars were flourishing and he walked slowly and contentedly back up Ice Tower Lane round the front of the church. Acting on an impulse he turned left and went along Priest Way instead of continuing up the High Street. Then he turned right into Leather Lane and walked into the pub, the Leather Bottle. I haven't seen William Tew for a month or two, he thought as he pushed open the door into the saloon bar and entered. It was early and the pub was empty. William Tew was polishing glasses in readiness for the evening. He looked up in surprise.

"Hello, my Lord," he said, "haven't seen you in here for a month or two. How are you keeping, Sir?"

Lord Bushden walked slowly across to the counter, lifted himself carefully on to the leather-covered stool. Truth to tell, he was glad to sit down, for the walk had tired him more than he had realized.

"Ah, William," he said, "no candle burns forever."

They talked together as friends for five minutes, but Lord Bushden rapidly saw that something was bothering William. He looked at him from beneath his bushy eyebrows. "Something on your mind, William," he said. "Out with it."

William looked embarrassed. "I don't hardly like to, my Lord," he said.

Lord Bushden beckoned impatiently. They'd known each other too long for holding back. This was the first inkling he had that Rupert Samuel was running the estate in a manner as different from the tradition he had established as charity is from kindness. The evening custom of the open door had ended abruptly. The dowries, the gifts to the village charities, had all stopped.

"I myself had a bit of a problem," William said. "In the old days I would have come up and talked it over with you. The brewery has been taken over by a young businessman."

"Lord Silsdon's finally retired?" Lord Bushden asked.

"Yes, and now the new people are making conditions I don't like. They've changed the beer . . ."

"Thought it tasted peculiar," Lord Bushden said.

". . . and I wanted to ask about turning this into a Free House and going somewhere else . . ."

"Quite right, too. If they're mucking about with the ale and trying to interfere in the selling of it, I should be inclined to give them a piece of my mind . . ."

"The licence is in your name, Lord Bushden," William gently reminded him. "I'm only your tenant."

Lord Bushden had been angered by what William had told him. Not so much the business about the brewery, but the larger issue of access to his own house. He had assumed that Rupert Samuel had been carrying on the traditions his father had accepted from his father before him. Of course, Rupert Samuel had modernized certain procedures like the cutting of timber and the acreage put down to plough, and had already started a plan to amalgamate some of the farms to make for easier working and more economic use of machinery. That sort of thing made sense. But not this petty and somewhat shoddy treatment of the villagers.

"Come up to the house tomorrow," Lord Bushden said, "about six o'clock if you can manage it. I shall arrange with Dobbs and Dobbs to hand the licence over to you and to put you in ownership. Then you can make your own decisions. Does that suit your book?" He looked at William from beneath his eyebrows again and slowly a smile crept across his face. William was unable to speak for gratitude. "We're getting long in the tooth, you and I, William," Lord Bushden said, "too long to have this kind of fence between us. Now how about a glass of whisky? This beer tastes horrible to my uneducated palate. And do me the honour of joining me in a glass."

That was the first time Lord Bushden realized that with his son's tremendous ability also went a cold ruthlessness, an extraordinary impersonality. He could remember how fastidious the boy had always been, how he'd never seemed to find many friends at school or university, how he'd never even brought a girl to the Hall. Of course, there had been girls about, the sisters of boys of similar families in the county, but Rupert Samuel had never attached himself to any one of them.

As Lord Bushden walked slowly home, warmed and stimulated by the whisky, he chuckled at the memory of a couple of "wild oats" he'd sown in his youth before Emily had finally captured his heart. He'd even maintained a young lady in St. James for a time. At the time it seemed deliciously wicked, the man-of-the-world thing to do, and he resolved to ask Rupert Samuel if he had ever indulged himself in that direction. Dammit, he thought, I don't know if the lad's ever bedded a gel . . .

Rupert's sole interest seemed to centre on the title and the estate, and the only other time recently that Lord Bushden had been angered was when Rupert Samuel insisted the title would not be safe preserved in the person of his older brother.

"There are steps you could take," Rupert said. "You could apply for a Lords Commission to examine the matter, and most probably the Letters Patent would be changed by Royal Decree. I consulted Wetherfold and Springer, the best solicitors for this sort of matter, and they're certain that a Royal Decree could be obtained."

Lord Bushden was angered that Rupert Samuel had seen fit to consult lawyers without first discussing the matter with him. "David Arthur is the first born," he said, "and the title is his by way of right. It's not his fault that his mental faculties are not equal to yours. Or that he's the picture of health. I shall leave him sufficient money always to be looked after and cared for, and the rest of the estate will come to you. The house, the grounds, the land, the farms, everything will be yours . . ."

"But the *title* will die out . . . ?"

"That's as may be." Both were silent. It was apparent to both that David Arthur should never marry. He could never take on the adult responsibilities of a marriage. It would be the end of a long line.

"Of course I know that," Lord Bushden had said gruffly. It had been a difficult decision to take and maintain all these years. He knew that lawyers can twist anything round, and no doubt the proviso could be expunged, or at least suspended, from the Letters Patent. But Lord Bushden would not expose David Arthur to that. No doubt there would have to be all sorts of reports from psychiatrists and doctors and lawyers, and the boy had already been through enough of that, thanks to his mother. Lord Bushden was determined; so long as David Arthur were alive, he'd take his rightful inheritance as first born, and nothing Rupert Samuel could say would make him change his mind. The title would die out; well, titles were an anachronism these days anyway, and what did Rupert Samuel need with one? He would be successful in the management of his considerable financial inheritance without all the pomp and panoply of a seat in the Lords.

That was the evening on which Lord Bushden took to his bed. Dr. Samson said the whisky had overexcited him, the walk had tired him, the tumour had reached its final stage. But when William Tew came the following day Lord Bushden's solicitors handed him the title and ownership of the Leather Bottle, and he became the only man, other than Lord Bushden, to own property in the village of Bushden. He knew then that the old man had lost his zest for life. He stood by the bedside and Lord Bushden clasped his hand. "An era is drawing to a close, William, he said. "Modern ways owe nothing to the past, nothing to the values you and I have both held so dear." There were tears in William's eyes as he gazed at the figure in the bed which seemed visibly to have shrunk since the previous evening. "Cain and Abel," his Lordship had said. "It was ever thus. One brother jealous of the other."

The nurse engaged by Dr. Samson tiptoed to the bedside. "I think you should go now, Mr. Tew," she said.

William walked from the room, realizing how much of a way of life, how much personal dignity and warm generosity he was leaving behind him.

"No, Sir. She had been released at her Ladyship's request, two days ago. Her Ladyship wanted to look after the Master."

"Anyone else in the house?"

"The two young Masters would be in their rooms dressing for dinner. I had given the staff permission to be absent. I knew that when the Master went, they would all be busy and this could be the last opportunity for a night off."

"Very understanding of you, Porter."

"You have to be careful with staff these days, Sir. Cook had gone shortly before the vicar arrived. Dinner is always a simple affair on Friday evenings, unless we are entertaining, and her Ladyship was always gracious enough to assist in the dining room."

"So far as you knew, no one was in the house but the two young masters, yourself, and Lord and Lady Bushden?"

"That is absolutely correct, Sir."

Aveyard walked up the steps to the master bedroom. Constable Rogers, standing outside the bedroom door, drew himself to attention when he saw the superintendent. He was holding his helmet beneath his arm and made as if to put it on but Aveyard greeted him and told him to stand easy. The constable cleared his throat. "Dr. Samson in, Sir, nobody out."

Aveyard smiled. Rogers was a bye-word on the Birton police force, with a round smiling face that had won him the nickname of Jolly. Where he was standing now, in front of the collection of swords which lined the upper hall, seemed quite appropriate, as if he were the custodian. He was leading bass in the police operatic society where his chief delight was the annual performance of Gilbert and Sullivan, especially when the repertoire included excerpts from the *Pirates of Penzance*. Jolly Rogers had nursed many a young constable through the start of his official career; he'd helped Aveyard himself out of a scrape or two. But no hint of familiarity crossed that rubicund face.

CHAPTER THREE

When Detective Superintendent Aveyard arrived at Bushden Hall Sergeant Jim Bruton was waiting for him by the front door. "Dr. Samson is here, Sir," he said, all official and on duty, "and he's hopping mad."

"It won't be the first time, Jim," Aveyard said. He walked into the hall. The butler was standing at the far end by a massive mahogany table. His fingertips rested lightly on its surface. Arthur Porter recognized a "superior" person when he saw one, walked forward, and stopped three yards from the superintendent, looking expectant.

"Arthur Porter," the sergeant said, "is the one who telephoned."

"I'd like to talk with you in detail later," Bill Aveyard said, "but I wonder if for the moment you could just repeat to me the exact words Lord Bushden used that caused you to telephone our office."

Arthur Porter thought for a moment. When he spoke his voice, despite his seventy years, was clear and precise. "His Lordship was speaking to the vicar at the time and I was a short distance away, but I believe I heard what his Lordship said. 'Fetch the police, there's a good man,' those were the exact words, of that I am quite sure."

"Who else was present at the time?"

"Her Ladyship was standing at the other side of the bed, the vicar at this side, and I had taken up my accustomed position beside the door, in case my services should be required. No one else was in the room."

"No nurse?"

Rogers opened the door and Aveyard went inside. Dr. Samson was standing beside the bed, a stethoscope hanging round his neck and his bag on the counterpane beside the body of Lord Bushden, whose dressing gown and pyjama jacket had been opened. As Aveyard came into the room he was using an ophthalmoscope to examine the pupil of one of Lord Bushden's eyes. Dr. Samson straightened up and glared across the bed at the superintendent.

"I can't see why we have to have all this nonsense," he said angrily. "The presence of the police here is causing unwarranted distress to this family." He bent and looked through the ophthalmoscope again. Aveyard walked to the bed slowly without speaking. Dr. Samson switched off the light of the instrument, placed it in its case and put it back inside his black medical bag. Then he stood erect, facing the superintendent across the bed. "Look here," he said, "this man has been my patient for thirty years or more. During that time I have seen him every week of my life, professionally or socially. He has died as a result of a brain tumour. I am perfectly convinced of that, and prepared to sign the Death Certificate. The law on that point is quite specific. I have been in daily attendance on my patient throughout his terminal illness. This patient has been seen during that time by specialists from Kettering and Northampton hospitals. My own partner saw him today at my request and is perfectly competent both medically and legally to countersign the Death Certificate which I have already prepared. And yet at the very moment of decease, when the family require peace and dignity, you march your heavy footed fellow to the door of this room, eject the widow from the bedside of her loved one and seal the place as tight as a vault. Now what have you to say for yourself, Detective Superintendent Aveyard?"

Bill looked across the bed at him. "That's quite a speech you've just made, Dr. Samson, and I agree with every word of it."

"Then why, man, why?"

"Let me ask you one small question," Aveyard said. "I am quite prepared to believe Lord Bushden has died of natural causes. I am happy to think that during the closing stages of his life he had the benefit of your medical services, but why were his last words—and here I quote the butler—*Fetch the police, there's a good man?*"

Dr. Samson didn't even consider his reply. "How the devil should I know that? A man dying, mind full of fantasy, man of great affairs, possibly remembered some small aberration in one of his businesses he thought needed correcting, probably some petty pilfering. How should I know? The man has died. I know how, I know why and I can go so far as to say I could almost have predicted when. Why do you think I asked my partner to come here today if not so that he could have last minute information to make the Death Certificate fully legal?"

Aveyard was shaking his head from side to side.

"Don't shake your head at me, you young whipper-snapper," Dr. Samson said, losing all reserve, all control. Detective Superintendent Aveyard was the youngest man of that rank on the Birton police force. Dr. Samson was a much respected general practitioner who for the last thirty years had also worked as a police surgeon in the district.

But young though he was, Aveyard knew his responsibilities. He stopped shaking his head. "I'm sorry, Dr. Samson," he said. "I appreciate everything you say, but Lord Bushden asked to see the police before he died. I have three unimpeachable witnesses to the fact and I intend to discover why. I agree with you that it may be nothing more serious than a case of petty pilfering; perhaps someone was helping himself to Lord Bushden's pheasants, or perhaps the licence of one of Lord Bushden's dogs needs renewing . . ."

"No need to be flippant," Dr. Samson said. He knew the superintendent was right, of course, but he had never been able to accustom himself to the medical intrusion that can follow a death once the police become involved. This was doubly so when the deceased was someone he had known personally and had tended with professional integrity. "I suppose that means an autopsy," he said.

Aveyard nodded. "John Victor is on duty tonight, and I've asked him to stand by."

Dr. Samson's face closed tight at the mention of that name. John Victor was a pathologist known for the thoroughness with which he conducted his investigations. There wouldn't be much of Lord Bushden left intact when John Victor had finished.

"How *can* you?" he asked. His hands rested on the shoulder of the deceased. "He'll need to open the head, you know."

"I know," Aveyard said, "and I don't welcome that any more than you do."

Dr. Samson drew his hand down the side of Lord Bushden's face. The features were reposed though the cheeks had sunk a little. In his death Lord Bushden carried all the dignity of his life. His white hair had been brushed back on his forehead, no doubt with the loving care of his lifelong friend and butler, Arthur Porter. Dr. Samson had closed Lord Bushden's eyes at the completion of his examination. The long eyelids and the long upper lip gave the face an aristocracy which survived even death. John Victor was no respecter of persons, both knew that, and Bill Aveyard had often faced this dilemma.

"I'm sorry, Dr. Samson," he said. "I'm truly sorry."

When Dr. Samson spoke again the anger had drained from him leaving behind an infinite sadness. "And so you should be," he said quietly, "so you should be."

Bill Aveyard left the bedroom and went downstairs. Lady Bushden was waiting for him in the morning room in which a fire had recently been lighted. She was sitting in a large armchair gazing into the flames. "We'll have to tell the boys," she said, "but the police officer to whom Porter spoke insisted we should do nothing until you arrived. Thank you very much for coming so quickly."

Porter had followed Aveyard into the room and anticipated her Ladyship's command. "Shall I bring them both together, your Ladyship, or would the gentleman prefer to see them separately?"

Aveyard didn't turn round, didn't address the butler directly. "I would rather see them separately, if that would be all right," he said.

She nodded. "Yes, that would be better. I don't know how much you know about our son David." She brought her hand quickly to her mouth and tears glistened in her eyes, though Aveyard knew nothing would permit her to shed them in his presence. "I suppose I should call him Lord Bushden now," she said.

"I know a little about your son," Aveyard said. "I think it would be better if we were to see your second son first. Perhaps he can help us to break the news to his brother."

"How very wise of you."

The butler left the morning room without any explicit command. Lady Bushden beckoned to a chair. "Won't you be seated," she said. "You'll have to forgive us, if things are a little out of the way."

He sat down and looked at her, waiting to discover if she wanted to talk. It had been his experience that bereavement can do one of two things to people: it can either make them silent or garrulous. Which would she be? He judged her to be in her late fifties. She was tall and thin and her face had a quality of serenity, as if she had never been caused to suffer deeply, or had learned to conceal it. Her hair was brown and elegantly coiffed; her dress of dark tweed had a stylish classic simplicity. She wore a plain gold band around her neck and on her fingers were a wedding ring and an engagement ring, a large diamond.

She crossed her knees in the chair, placed her hands along its arms and pushed herself back into it as if feeling a need for its familiar comfort. "I've often thought of this moment recently," she said, "but I'm afraid I've not been able to work out how to face it. Quite simply, a part of my life has ended. My husband was everything to me, and I do not know how I shall continue without him. But of course, the boys need me and I shall continue to do my best for them." She gave a nervous laugh. "Do forgive me," she said, "I'm afraid I'm talking rather a lot." Aveyard did not know what to say, wished he had thought to bring a policewoman with him, or that Jim Bruton was by his side ready to respond as he always did. Aveyard, no doubt still nettled by Samson's use of the word "whippersnapper," felt too young for his job and its many responsibilities.

"I'm sure your sons need you," he said, "and you'll find a great comfort in looking after them."

The door opened and the butler entered.

"Excuse me, Lady Bushden," he said, "but I think the gentleman should come upstairs. There has been a terrible tragedy." His composure broke, tears rained down his cheeks, and he so forgot himself as to turn to the superintendent and address him directly. "It's Mr. Rupert Samuel, Sir," he said. "He's dead."

Lady Bushden sat still in her chair, still as Lot's wife.

"What's that you say, Porter?" she whispered.

"Mr. Rupert Samuel, my Lady. I fear he's dead."

Aveyard was already out of his chair. He went across and stood in front of her, his eyes examining her quickly but carefully. "You all right?" She nodded. She turned her head and her eyes sought those of Porter, beseechingly. He nodded gravely.

"Yes, my Lady, I'm afraid it's true."

She brought her hand up to her mouth and her voice was muffled by her knuckles as she said, "Go and do what you must do. I shall stay here. I couldn't bear to see him. Go and do what you must do."

Bill Aveyard ran quickly up the stone steps and Bruton

followed. "Get Dr. Samson," he said. The butler in the hall below was pointing to the left of the upstairs hall, along the gallery. Aveyard opened the door, went inside, and found himself in the sitting room of a set of private apartments. An open door on the right revealed a bedroom beyond and a door next to it, also open, gave on to a dressing room. To the left inside an alcove was a small kitchenette and beyond that a bathroom.

Rupert Samuel was lying on the carpet in the centre of the sitting room, wearing evening pumps, evening dress trousers and what had been a white shirt. On the carpet beside him was a long flat-bladed sword with a green velvet-decorated handle. The blade of the sword was covered in blood; blood had stained the white shirt and a large pool of it had run into the cream-coloured carpet on which the body lay. A blow had been struck on the side of the neck and Aveyard suspected from the amount of blood spilled that the jugular vein had been severed.

The door behind him opened again as Dr. Samson and Jim Bruton came into the room. Both were too experienced to walk across the carpet; they stood next to Bill Aveyard while he surveyed the scene. All Dr. Samson's antagonism had gone.

He put a hand on Bill Aveyard's arm. "I'm dreadfully sorry," he said, "you appear to have been right." He looked at the corpse lying on the carpet. "What a dreadful thing, what a dreadful thing for Lady Bushden. We shall have to find David Arthur before he can do anything else."

Aveyard turned quickly to him. "Why do you say that?"

"You know the boy is simple-minded. Such an act of savagery . . ."

"You said *simple*-minded. It's not the same thing."

"I know, but it's fair to assume . . ."

"It's fair to *assume* nothing . . ." Aveyard was angry. He turned again and surveyed the scene, his mind working rap-

Idly. "Fact, Dr. Samson, that's what I want. Not assumptions.
Is he dead?"

"Yes, of course. I can see that even from here."

"Right." He turned to Bruton. "We'll have John Victor up
here," he said, "and you better get the boys."

"I've already told Rogers to make the call. They should be
on their way. I had them standing by in case you needed
them for Lord Bushden." Aveyard looked gravely at him.
Trust Jim Bruton with his mind like a computer to have
started the police procedures. "I'll warn Rogers about Mr.
Victor," Bruton said as he left the room.

If there can be such a thing this was an ideal scene on which
to conduct a murder investigation. Unimpeded by members
of the public, by weather conditions, by the need for ordinary life to continue, the room could be sealed while the
forensic experts examined it in great detail, sifting the information they would find. The body need not be moved until
it had yielded all the knowledge of which it was capable.
Dr. Samson, acting as police surgeon, had already fulfilled
his prime function, that of certifying that life had ended.
Now the victim passed out of the care of medicine into the
cold laboratory of forensic science.

"Do you want me to do an examination, take body temper-
ature readings and so on?" Samson asked, but Aveyard shook
his head.

"John Victor will be here soon enough for that and I'd
rather not have anybody walk over that carpet until he's
been." Aveyard looked at the sword which logically at this
moment he dare not assume might be the murder weapon.
"Look at that wretched handle," he said. "We'll never get a
print off that."

"If you don't need me?" Dr. Samson asked. Aveyard nodded and Dr. Samson left the room. I never saw a woman
who less needed her doctor, he thought to himself, thinking
again of Lady Bushden's composure. Alone and in the dark-

ness of the night she might yield to human temptation and shed a few silent tears, but no man living would ever witness the breakdown of that imperious composure. Aveyard stood still and looked about him, mopping up impressions like a sponge.

Rupert Samuel had been a precise and meticulous young man, that was apparent at once, even allowing for the attention of servants. Nothing in the apartment was out of place, nothing had been put down casually, without purpose. Aveyard thought of his own apartment, his tennis racket hanging behind the door, his shoes higgledy piggledy in the bottom of the wardrobe, his jackets not always set on hangers in the wardrobe. He thought of all the charivari of everyday life and could see none of it, no visual evidence that anybody had ever lived a careless existence within these walls. From where he was standing he could see the meticulous order of the bedroom and the dressing room. It can't all be done by servants, he thought.

He went to the door, took out his handkerchief, used it to grasp the shank of the ornate doorhandle and pulled the door open. Porter was still standing in the lower hall waiting like a gun dog for further instructions. Aveyard beckoned him to come upstairs.

"If it's all the same to you, Sir," Porter said, "I'd rather not go back into that room unless you require me to do so."

Aveyard patted the old man's arm. "No, Porter," he said, "I shan't ask you to do that, but what I would like you to do is to talk to me, rather quickly if you can, about Mr. Rupert Samuel. Tell me what sort of a man he was. I know this is painful for you, but it will help me considerably. You see, my task is to discover whoever is responsible and I'm sure you will want to help me do that."

The old man nodded. "Yes," he said, "I'm afraid we must do that."

Aveyard was quick to seize the word. "Afraid, Porter," he said, "why afraid?"

Porter looked beseechingly at him. "Mr. David Arthur," he said hesitantly.

"Porter, I want you to put Mr. David Arthur right out of your mind. The law of England says no man is guilty until that fact has been proven in court. I can't conduct an investigation on the assumption that one man is guilty. Now, no more about Mr. David Arthur. Tell me about Mr. Rupert Samuel."

Porter began slowly but the information came tumbling from him, a complete account of the man Rupert Samuel was becoming. Without Porter meaning to be censorious or disloyal, the picture he painted was of a hard, cruel young man with none of the understanding and kindness of his father, a man without friends or intimates who lived his life selfishly, bereft of human emotion.

"I hope you won't think it amiss of me to mention one point," Porter said, "but I didn't like the way he got rid of the dogs. The dogs were Lord Bushden's pride and joy. Basset hounds. We had twenty of them. Lord Bushden used to call them "the pack" and liked nothing better than to walk through the grounds with them running around him. He refused to have them trained, wouldn't even keep a kennel man. Amanda Tew—her father runs the public house in the village—used to look after them and she was very fond of them. I was too, though I'm not one to care much for domestic animals. But the day after Lord Bushden took to his bed, Mr. Rupert Samuel called in the vet and had every last one of them put to sleep. It broke Miss Tew's heart, I can tell you. Of course, it wasn't my place to say anything about it, but I happened to overhear when Miss Tew asked him why and he said, and I'm afraid I didn't take kindly to it, "Basset hounds, Miss Tew, are very uneconomical.'"

Porter looked at Aveyard and gave one of the little coughs with which Aveyard was becoming familiar. It meant that what Porter was about to say exceeded the bounds of propriety. "Miss Tew, you see, Sir, was always very good with Mr.

David Arthur and you might say she looked after him as carefully as she looked after the basset hounds, and if you forgive me for saying so, Sir, I think Mr. Rupert Samuel was perhaps just a little bit jealous of Mr. David Arthur and Miss Tew. The hounds were his way of scoring a point. But you understand, that's only my personal observation."

"How close were the two brothers," Aveyard said.

Now that Porter had committed one indiscretion Aveyard guessed others would be forthcoming. He was not mistaken.

"You'll allow me to speak my mind, Sir, but I always thought Mr. Rupert Samuel was a little two-faced about Mr. David Arthur. He always seemed very friendly, you understand. Mr. David Arthur was never difficult, just, shall we say, childish, and it sometimes seemed to me that Mr. Rupert Samuel didn't really like him. Of course, when they were boys together, it was even worse and several times I had to exceed my station and intervene and even chide Mr. Rupert Samuel for being cruel to his brother. Once he locked him in the game room with one of the gun dogs and the gun dog went wild. That upset Mr. David Arthur terribly and he even broke a window to get out. Of course, they used to spend a lot of time together. They used to disappear for hours and we never knew where they were. One of their favourite hiding places was the priest hole—you know we have a priest hole here off the orangery—but I always knew where to look when they had disappeared from view."

Further reminiscences from Porter were abruptly cut short when the front door bell rang. He hurried down the steps and let in Sergeant Bruton, who had been waiting outside for the arrival of John Victor, the pathologist, and the forensic team. They came up the steps carrying their equipment, cameras, lights, plastic containers, and finally a long wooden box. Aveyard opened the door of the room and gave his instructions tersely.

"Usual shots of the room and the body," he said to the camera man, "full plate black and white and 35mm. colour."

He turned to the fingerprint man. "I haven't touched the inside of the door," he said, "but I imagine the butler has. He'll give you a list of the people with access to the room for comparison prints. All the staff is out this evening so you'll need to wait until they get back." He turned back to the camera man. "A sword in there," he said, "with a green velvet handle. I'd like a full close-up of that handle, something we can blow up really big. Oblique lighting and shots all the way round. I don't think we'll get anything out of it, but it's worth a try."

He turned to John Victor. "Dr. Samson's here," he said. "He certified death and we haven't been anywhere near the body. The only other man in the room, I suspect, since it took place is the butler, but you never know."

John Victor was wearing rimless pince-nez spectacles which seemed to enlarge his eyeballs. His brown hair was brushed back meticulously. He was wearing a smock in plain blue lintless linen, a pair of plain blue linen trousers. On his feet, incongruously one might have thought if one didn't know his job, he wore a pair of American basketball boots. He took a skull cap in plain blue linen from his pocket and put it on his head to cover his hair. From his pocket he also took a pair of rubber gloves in a plastic bag. He tore off the plastic and put on the rubber gloves.

"Don't tell me you've given me a clean job for once," he said humourlessly.

Aveyard smiled at him. "It's as clean as a new pin," he said, "and it's all yours."

The pathologist pushed the door open with his rubberclad fingertips and stood looking at the scene. Then he bent down and pulled a pair of linen overshoes over his basketball boots. He looked like something out of a Television Doctor series of 1984, but Aveyard knew his fastidiousness was justified. John Victor was going to be looking for grains of dust and drops of blood, for microscopic fibres, hairs, all the minute traces a murderer must inevitably leave at the scene of his crime.

"He's dead right enough," he said. "Even a first-year student could tell you that."

"Yes," Aveyard said, "but who killed him?"

"That's your affair, not mine. I hope to be able to tell you how and where and when, and with what. Who and why is your business, not mine." John Victor turned to the forensic team. "Let's get to work. We don't want him to go cold on us."

CHAPTER FOUR

The entrance to the old Vicarage was just below where the High Street joined Nether Way South, and just above Ice Tower Lane. Aveyard and Bruton went under the fourteenth-century porch together walking purposefully, saying nothing. The old vicarage was three storeys high and an old stone building that looked solid and lived in. There were lights behind the curtains of the ground floor and a light on what must have been the first-floor landing that shone through a stained-glass window ten or more feet high. In a small abutment to the side of the house a central heating boiler rumbled quietly; there was no other noise. Aveyard pulled the bell hanging beside the large nail-encrusted door and from within he heard the incongruous peal of tinny handbells. They didn't have long to wait; the door opened and a tiny old lady stood there, her face scrubbed white as an altar cloth, her silver hair pulled severely down the sides of her face and tied at the back in a no-nonsense bun. She was wearing a black dress and over it a starched white apron. Her flat-heeled shoes were black and had clumpy toes. She could have come equally well from a hospital of charity or a Rembrandt painting. When she spoke her voice was soft and diffident, as if apologizing for the noise it made.

"Is the vicar at home?" Aveyard said. He felt he ought to have crossed himself first. The hand she laid on the door to open it wider was red with scrubbing soap and her spatulate nails were almost transparent as if they'd lain too long in bleach.

"I'll see, Sir," she said. "Who shall I tell him is calling?"

"Superintendent Aveyard and Sergeant Bruton," Jim Bruton said.

She gave a little bob and was visibly impressed. "Oh dear," she said, "you'd better come in and I'll get him right away." She showed them into a room beside the front door which smelled of soap, beeswax, and dead chrysanthemums, though of course there were no such flowers to be seen. In the corner of the room was a Monstera Delicosa, its large indented leaves polished to a bright green and bowed as if in prayer. Next to it was a brass-bound Bible on an old oak reading stand. It was open at Deuteronomy II. A picture on the wall above the black marble fireplace was the reproduction of a page of the Gutenberg Bible. The woman waited until they had seated themselves and she went out of the room again, bobbing like a cork. They were left alone. Aveyard looked about him.

"This is the sort of place you'd expect to hear organ music on Musak," he said, but Bruton merely grunted, obviously ill at ease.

The vicar came in, tall and hearty, dry washing his hands. "Oh yes, the police!" he said, "what can I do for you?" His voice had the lightness of gossamer and was just as thin.

Sergeant Bruton grunted again.

Aveyard got up, motioned to Bruton to stay where he was. He gave their names and the vicar nodded wisely. He got the feeling the vicar would nod wisely if Aveyard said he was God Almighty come to check up on how the vicar was doing.

"I understand that shortly before his death Lord Bushden said some words to you. I'd be grateful if you could repeat those words to me as exactly as you can remember them."

"Ah yes! Lord Bushden! Some words! Well, I'm not too sure if I can remember them exactly. The death of a beloved person is always attended with a certain emotion, you understand? Although of course we must remember the Lord

God chooses his own time to take us and sees fit in His merciful Way to draw unto Himself His beloved servants.'

"What did he *say?*"

"Ah yes, actually what he did say was, and I think I can remember the words because they seemed at the time to be rather strange and not the sort of thing you would expect Lord Bushden to concern himself with at a time when he knew his soul was going to meet His Maker . . ."

Sergeant Bruton grunted again. "If you could just tell us the *words*, Sir," he said, getting to his feet. "I think you can safely take it we've both been to Bible class."

The vicar was stopped in mid flight. "Ah yes, the *words*. Well, what he actually said was . . ." He paused. "I mean, do you want all of it or just the last bit, because we had a complete conversation, you understand."

"I think we'd better have all of it," Aveyard said gravely.

"Well, when I went into the room Lord Bushden said something I couldn't quite make out and so he said 'Didn't you hear me, Vicar?' and so I said 'I didn't quite catch what you said, my Lord,' and he said something like—you understand, don't you, that I'm trying to remember exactly what it was because I know how important the actual words are for police work—you have to have the exact phrasing because a word, just a word, no doubt can make all the difference."

"Yes, it can," Aveyard said. "I think it would be better if you just confine yourself at this moment to repeating exactly what Lord Bushden said about the police. I have a method that will help you. Think exactly what those words were. No, don't say anything; just think what they were. When my sergeant says, 'now,' just say them. Nothing else. Just the words Lord Bushden used that caused you to tell the butler to send for the police. All right, start thinking now."

Sergeant Bruton almost laughed out loud. It was a technique Aveyard used to stop a garrulous witness. It never failed. He waited until the vicar's face looked composed.

"Now," he barked.

"Cain and Abel . . . it was ever thus . . . fetch the police . . . there's a good man." The words came out of the vicar as if fired from a machine gun and both Aveyard and Bruton heaved a sigh of relief.

"Cain and Abel . . . it was ever thus . . . fetch the police . . . there's a good man. Those were the exact words?" Aveyard asked.

"So far as I can remember," the vicar said.

Aveyard and Bruton were silent, both racking their brains to recall the Bible story of Cain and Abel, both reluctant to ask the vicar to expound, knowing they would never be able to dam the flow of words. Cain and Abel. Two brothers. One jealous of the other. One killed the other, but neither Bruton nor Aveyard could have said which one killed which.

"Have you any idea why Lord Bushden should ask you to fetch the police?" Aveyard asked.

"None whatsoever; I can assure you it came as a complete surprise to me. You could say I was shocked, even horrified, at the thought that his Lordship should spend the last moments of his life thinking about such a subject when he might properly concern himself with the Life to which he was going. It's a very grievous matter when a man dies without that serene calm the knowledge of the waiting arms of the Lord should bestow."

Here we go again, Bruton thought and remembered irreverently a remark Sergeant Hawkins had made one afternoon in the police canteen; he'd said, "Religion would be all right if they didn't keep bringing God into it!"

Aveyard persisted. "I'm not so much concerned at this moment," he said, "with the religious aspect of Lord Bushden's last moments on this earth, though I realize of course the need for thought about them. Can you think in a secular way for a moment? You knew Lord Bushden, the man, as distinct from the Lord Bushden who was one of your parishioners. Can you think of any reason why Lord Bushden, the man, should need to consult the police? It often happens,

you must have met it many times, that before his death a
man needs to confess to some crime he's committed, some
knowledge he possesses of an illegal act as distinct from an
immortal act. Can you think of anything in the life of Lord
Bushden that he would want to tell me."

The vicar was shaking his head. "It's quite inconceivable
to me," he said, "that his Lordship could ever commit any
act however small outside the convention of the Law. He
was a man at all times of the utmost probity. I cannot
believe that he would ever permit or condone any act of ille-
gality however small, however expedient."

"Why do you think he wanted to talk to the police?"

The vicar shook his head. "I just do not know," he said.
"I'm afraid I cannot be any help to you at all."

Aveyard knew he had to take the plunge. "What do you
think he meant by his reference to Cain and Abel?" he said.

The vicar looked at each of them in turn. "I can see this is
neither the time nor the place for a theological discussion.
You're both busy men."

"I know it will shock you," Aveyard said, "and I apologize
for having to give you such news so bluntly but would it also
surprise you to learn that Rupert Samuel has been killed?"

"Dear God," the vicar said. "Dear God." He looked at
Aveyard. "Would you mind awfully if I sit down." He sat in
a chair, visibly shaken by the news. "Cain and Abel becomes
quite clear to me," he said. "Lord Bushden must have
known. He'd want to tell the police, of course, even though
it was his own son."

"The dead boy . . ."

"No, the one who killed him."

CHAPTER FIVE

Friday evening in the village, and the elm trees rustled in a vagrant wind. Young men bathed in gas-fired hot water and rubbed Eau de Cologne into their skulls, humming and grinding their pelvic bones into the insides of their slim hipster trousers. Young girls wiped high platform block shoes with bathsponges and remembered to take the pill. Old women scooped meat and potatoes and green peas onto plates and looked anxiously at the television waiting for the start of programmes that reflected Life. Old men sat, head in hands, staring sightlessly out of the window reluctant to draw the curtains, remembering young summers and younger gaiety, fearing the arthritic pains that would come in the long night ahead.

A village rustles on a Friday evening like crushed chestnut leaves and the weekend stretches clear through the bell ringing Sabbath. William Tew polished glasses in the pub, looked around for the hundredth time and thought in wonderment, It's mine, it's all mine. Martha Tew set bags of peanuts like a supply column and touched her husband's forearm in gratitude for a good life. Fred Latham served cigarettes and sugar in the shop to latecomers who refused to let him close at six. Sally Latham took his dinner off the table and popped it back into the oven to keep warm.

Friday night's neither here nor there, not like Saturday. Boys and girls love Saturday night; mums and dads like Friday, remembering the time they took the bus into the Birton market to bring back bargains. Paul Kranceck shuffled papers unintelligible to anyone in the village but himself. Memento mori of his Polish ancestry, bought for mere coins in book markets. Old deeds, titles, stories, legends, old music, songs, anthems, litanies. Comfort to a man expatriated by a war he had not understood.

The Reverend Thomas Dalgleish flitted in the church like a swallow, dusting, tidying, rubbing, polishing, straightening, caring for a value that had perished. Friday night's a secular night; no services, marriages, births, only the death of Lord Bushden to sustain him. As he swooped his mind was active, thinking out the details of the ceremony for the interment of his patron. In the back of his mind lay a black grain of misgiving. Rupert Samuel was not like his father. When Rupert Samuel took control of the village much that had been lingering in a slow and inconceivable death would be consumed quickly on the pyre of modernity.

In the tall uncut grass at the bottom of West Farm a pheasant leaped cawking into the air, frightened by a footfall.

"What was that?" a young voice said.

"Only a bird."

"I could do with a bird right now."

"Not that kind of bird, you fool."

The beast was standing almost in the hedgerow pulling at the long grass, taking it slowly into its mouth and munching with a soft sucking sound. The beast lifted its head and looked indifferently at the two blackclad figures which approached, stalking beneath the shelter of the hedge. The first held out a fearful timid hand and stroked the beast's long bony nose. The beast rubbed his nose along the man's hand but continued to munch. The other figure came round the side of the beast and confidently pulled its ears. The beast loved that. It loved it when the man scratched the top of its head between its ears with the plate of the humane killer, before he pulled the trigger.

"Where's Porter?" Aveyard said to Jim Bruton. Now the hordes of investigating policemen were coming in and out of the front door, which was being left open. Aveyard could see past Bruton the half dozen or more vehicles parked in the drive outside the house. Bruton saw the direction of Aveyard's glance.

"I took the liberty of asking Lady Bushden if we could set up an Incidents Room," Bruton said. "She offered me the dining room; it's like the Albert Hall in there, but I think it'll do. Porter asked me if he could be excused for five minutes, and I've let him go into the village."

"You sent somebody with him, I hope."

"Jolly Rogers. He'll keep him happy."

"Who've we got for incidents officer?"

"Inspector Roberts of B Division. They wanted to send Charley Parker, but you know what he's like, he'd litter the place with fag ends. Roberts likes a touch of royalty. He'll break his back bowing Lords and Ladies."

At that moment the figure of a girl could be seen making her way through the chaos of the drive. She was tall, blonde and in her late twenties, Aveyard would have said. Arthur Porter and Constable Rogers were following about thirty paces behind; it was obvious the girl wanted to arrive as quickly as possible and could not wait for them. She was wearing a pair of drill riding trousers and a thick green polo neck sweater. Her hair was caught back behind her head in a no-nonsense pony tail and her face looked as though it had never seen Max Factor or any of his products. On her feet she wore gusseted brown leather hacking boots and Aveyard wondered for the moment where she had left her riding crop. She opened her mouth to speak and mentally he closed his ears, expecting a hunting call of gale force proportions, but the sound which issued was surprisingly soft and warm. "Can you direct me to Superintendent Aveyard?" she said. "I'm told he is a young looking man."

Aveyard caught the smile on Bruton's face, but turned towards the girl and said, "I'm Superintendent Aveyard and let me make a guess, you are Miss Amanda Tew." Bruton's jaw dropped and Aveyard noted that too with considerable satisfaction.

The girl looked at him coolly. "How could you possibly know that?" she said.

Aveyard smiled at her. "No magic, and I'm not clairvoyant. Mr. Porter has told me how kind you have been in the past. After the shock Mr. Porter has just had, I imagine he wanted to have you close by when we go looking for Mr. David Arthur."

"Poor Mr. Porter," she said. "He's so upset. How kind of you to send the constable to keep him company."

Now Bruton was smiling. "We like to be understanding, Miss," he said, wearing his Sunday solemn voice, not daring to look at Aveyard.

"I'm afraid I don't know much about what's going on," she said, "but of course I'll be happy to help any way I can. Mr. Porter has told me Lord Bushden has died. We all expected that, of course, and the whole village will be sorry. But then Mr. Porter said something about a tragedy and Mr. Rupert Samuel and would I come. Frankly he wasn't making much sense so I thought I'd better get over here as quickly as I could."

Aveyard looked at Amanda Tew, assessing her, trying to work out in his mind what sort of girl she might turn out to be. She didn't appear fluttery and female; she had a firm decisive quality that he knew could be a great asset in helping him to a deeper knowledge of the cross-currents within this house. After all, she'd worked here and looked the sort of girl to keep her eyes and ears open and her mouth shut. And hadn't Porter said how good she had been with David Arthur? "Look," he said, "I want you to help me. With your permission I'll not mince my words. Lord Bushden has died. The doctor who knows him . . ."

"Dr. Samson . . . ?"

"Yes, Dr. Samson, says the death is natural. Lord Bushden asked to see the police however, before he died. I want to know why. Secondly Mr. Rupert Samuel has been killed. The circumstances, which I won't trouble you with, clearly indicate murder . . ."

"And you think David Arthur might have done it?" she said.

"This is where I need your help. Everybody so far has reacted the way you have. You see, there was a reference to Cain and Abel and everybody's read the Bible. It's tempting to take the easy way and believe David Arthur is guilty—everybody assumes David Arthur must have been the one to kill his brother. I want to keep an absolutely open mind and I want you to help me by keeping an open mind yourself. Mr. Porter thinks David Arthur is in his room. Frankly, I don't believe that. There's been so much noise in this house in the last thirty minutes that he could not still be unaware of it. I think we'll have to go looking for him and when we find him I'd like you to be there. But not if you're going to assume he has killed his brother."

"You can rest assured about that. Look, Superintendent, I know David Arthur perhaps better than anybody else. He's only three years older than me, and I've been with him all my life. From the very earliest day he and I have been good friends. I know jolly well he hasn't killed anybody. I know jolly well he couldn't kill anybody, though I'm bound to say he's had every provocation from that brother of his. Oh, I know one should never speak ill of the dead, but I'm only saying now what I've told Rupert Samuel to his face a score of times."

By now the butler had regained his breath and was standing five yards to the side of them listening to every word. She turned. "You can vouch for that, can't you, Mr. Porter?"

He stepped forward and gave one of his little coughs. "Yes I can, Miss Tew," he said, "though we must try to think kindly."

They searched the house and the grounds and when they could find no trace of David Arthur Bushden Aveyard put out a call to Birton which spread instantaneously throughout the entire country. "David Arthur Bushden, age 30, height 5 feet 11 inches, hair brown, eyes hazel, no distinguishing scars, last seen wearing a green thornproof suit made by Airey and Wheeler with name inscribed in pocket. Handmade leather brogue walking shoes. Simple-minded, not known to be dangerous but take all care. Wanted to assist our inquiries, could be carrying a quantity of money, known to be fond of motor cars, but unable to drive. Also fond of trains and mechanical toys."

Aveyard, Porter and Amanda Tew had examined the Priests' Hole together. The entrance was located behind the panelling of a corridor wall that led to the Orangery. The mechanism was a simple spring loaded section of the dowelling, which only worked when a portion of the panelling was also pressed. The Priests' Hole was a chamber fifteen feet by six, with a stone flagged floor over which an old carpet had been laid. The interior walls were covered in random timber boards. Air came through a chimney in one corner, and there was a sink, an ancient tap for water, even a primitive lavatory pedestal which drained into a cess pit beneath the Orangery. In one corner of the room a construction had been made to act as a bed, and the ceiling was blackened by lamp and candle soot. Now an electric light had been installed, no doubt for the boys' convenience.

Aveyard stood in the centre of the room and, despite its warmth, he shivered, imagining all the priests for whom the room had been built in secrecy, sitting here day after day, night after night, knowing the terrible fate that awaited them if they were discovered or betrayed. He thought of the boys who had played here; the vicious one and the simpleton.

"They would never let me come in here," Amanda said. "It was their secret place. Once David Arthur tried to smuggle me in when Rupert Samuel was not about, but Rupert Samuel discovered us, and later tied his brother's wrists together. He was a devil, that one." She shuddered when she remembered.

Porter was standing still, and suddenly his face went white. He clutched Amanda Tew's arm and pointed.

"He's been in here," Porter said, "that was one of his favourites." It was a small furry teddy bear with a round black button for its navel. One eye had disappeared, and the fur was threadbare. When Porter pulled the navel button, it came away from the teddy bear, attached to a wire about ten inches long. When he let go of the button, the wire slowly wound back into the teddy bear's navel and a mechanism inside played "Happy Birthday."

"I gave it to him," Amanda said. "For his twenty-first birthday. Mr. Porter helped me to pick it."

CHAPTER SIX

"What do you think, Jim?" Bill Aveyard asked. They were standing outside the Hall in the darkness, the only light the beams from the rooms in which they could see men moving about. Bill Aveyard and Jim Bruton had worked together for many years and though they were of completely different temperaments, each complemented the other perfectly. Bruton had known Aveyard when he was an inspector and had watched him slowly mature as he grew into the greater responsibility of being a superintendent. Aveyard, he knew, relied heavily on instinct and feeling, using his mind and his brain as much as his eyes. Bruton always tried to back him up by having information at his fingertips. He was a desk and paper man, and his career had been spent searching for the provable fact. He was used to Aveyard asking what he thought and knew the last thing the younger man wanted was speculation.

He buttoned his overcoat tightly and hunched his shoulders into its warmth. Bill Aveyard, as usual, was wearing a windproof anorak and didn't seem to feel the cold. "Very little known," Bruton said, "but there very rarely is at the start, is there? Lord Bushden has died, and the first son is missing. The parson remembers Cain and Abel and blames the first son; for that matter, so does everybody else. All I can say is, it's a rum do, and that's for sure. As we both know, once you lift the lid off these old families you often find a can of worms." He was talking for talking's sake, providing Aveyard with a background for his thoughts.

Aveyard scuffed the ground with his toe. "I have a feeling

that all the evidence—I can't call it evidence—that all the *signs* point to the first son. First son kills second son. Dammit, from all acounts it was justified, since the brother was a bastard to him. Dad finds out, sends for police. Could be as simple as that. But it smells wrong to me."

"House to house? Find out if anybody has seen David Arthur in or around the village this evening. Stir it up a bit?"

"Can't do any harm, and I know the lads would welcome a bit of overtime coming up to Christmas."

Bruton stared at the house for a moment. "One thing," he said. "I don't know if there is anything in it, but has it struck you that it's remarkably empty for a house that size? Should be a lot more people bustling about, shouldn't there? You know, agents, servants, gardeners, all that sort of thing. Do you think anybody could have got rid of them deliberately?"

Aveyard opened his arms in a futile gesture. "Anything is possible, though the butler says he gave them all the night off."

At that moment the main door opened and Inspector Roberts stood on the doorstep beneath the portico looking out. "We're here," Aveyard called. They walked to where the inspector waited.

"All set up," he said. "The house has three telephone lines and the post office has given us two. The two numbers are jumped back into the remaining line. The van's on its way with our stuff. The forensic team has finished its preliminaries and Mr. Victor says you can come up now, if you want to."

Aveyard and Bruton walked slowly up the stone stairs. There was no sign of Lady Bushden, but two girls stood at the back of the downstairs hall, whispering together. Rogers was standing beside them. He made a move as if to approach the superintendent but Bruton shook his head and Rogers stayed where he was.

Inside the room a plastic sheet had been laid from the

door and all round the corpse. John Victor's specimen box
stood on a side table and Aveyard could see most of the bottles it contained were already labelled. He knew they'd be
samples of blood from the corpse, from the sword, and from
the carpet, and that within an hour John Victor would verify
or deny that they came from the same source.

"I haven't moved the body yet," John Victor said. "I
haven't needed to. Do you want first impressions?"

Aveyard said yes.

John Victor stood near the corpse. "I think the assailant
stood in front of his victim with the sword either held up in
the air or carried on his shoulder. The victim was upright.
The assailant was approximately the same size as the victim.
Only one blow was struck, but the sword is sharp and heavy
and not much force would be required. I'll give you details
of that later. The blow severed the jugular vein—you don't
want a lot of scientific jargon, I imagine? The victim would
of course start to spurt blood and in fact I've found where
the blood landed." He pointed to a spot on the carpet. "The
victim must have stood absolutely still after the blow was
struck, because I can find only one area into which the blood
spurted. If he'd moved about or staggered around the blood
would have been everywhere. I imagine he went immediately into deep shock; death would be quick and he would
drop where he stood. You'll notice the position of the knees,"
he said, pointing down at the corpse, "is entirely in accord-
ance with a straight fall, not a dive forward or a stagger
backwards. Also," he said, "if you look at the trajectory of
the spurted blood you see that too conforms to this thought.
Of course, I haven't done anything more than a superficial
examination, but I would judge the victim was a man in reasonable health, though not one to take exercise. A lot of sub-
cutaneous fatty tissue on the neck and the face suggests he
was not given to an outdoor life. No immediate evidence of
any other cause of death though again I emphasize this is

only a superficial examination, and we'll know more when I
look at the organs. I think, however, we can safely say he
was killed by a blow from the sword, which the assailant
then dropped beside the victim. Again, a pattern of blood
drops where the sword hit the carpet confirms that fact. I
lifted the sword briefly but I've put it back where it was and
the blade is outlined in blood drops on the carpet. We
should have some very good photographs of that for you. In
fact, we couldn't have a better medium than this cream
coloured carpet." John Victor's voice had been cold and
precise. He could have been describing a block of wood to a
group of carpenters. Bill Aveyard welcomed that; the brush
with Dr. Samson had left a nasty taste in his mouth.

"How long can I have before you move him?" Aveyard
asked.

John Victor shrugged his shoulders. "If you're satisfied
with my diagnosis of the cause of death," he said, "you can
have him as long as you need." He looked at a watch pinned
to the inside of the top pocket of his smock. "Mind you, I
like to get to bed before breakfast time if I can."

"Give me fifteen minutes," Aveyard said. "Two girls are
waiting at the back of the hall downstairs, probably servants. I'll bet Inspector Roberts has already organized them
to make a cup of tea. Take the lads with you."

The forensic team had packed most of their instruments
and they left the room with the pathologist. Aveyard and
Bruton were alone with the corpse. Aveyard bent down and
examined it. He could see what John Victor had meant;
Rupert Samuel had been going to fat, a roly poly man. The
wound was simple, but deadly. No man could survive a blow
like that. Aveyard looked at the sword. The edge was keen
and the sword heavy. It would not take much effort to wield
such a thing effectively. Then he walked around the apartment, touching nothing, looking at everything, pho-
tographing everything in his mind. Rupert Samuel had ob-

viously used this room as a private office as well as his living
quarters. The bookcase between the two windows contained
works of estate and business management, no light novels,
no frivolous biographies, no story books of adventure. Beneath the bookcase an elegant mahogany storage cabinet
with deep wide shelves carried backnumbers of the *Financial Times* and the *Economist*. Along the right-hand wall
was a writing bureau in solid wood, but it contained no love
letters, no card or word games. On the left was a portable
electric typewriter, on the right an electric adding machine
and calculator. The writing bureau was open and on the
green leather fold-down shelf stood an electronic pocket
calculator. Each compartment of the writing desk had
been labelled. Aveyard read Bank, Timber, Daily Returns,
Monthly Reports, Financial Summary, Analyses.

He went through to the bedroom. The walls were covered
with heraldic drawings and genealogies of the Bushden family tree, in every detail. There were no other pictures. The
headboard of the bed contained built-in shelves and several
volumes. Aveyard noted *Who's Who* and *Burke's Peerage*.
To the left of the bed head was a small bookcase on which
stood Goldberg's five volume *Summary of the Law for Estate Managers*. It was bound in moroccan leather. Five look-
alike navy blue striped suits in the dressing room, a drawer
which contained a dozen identical white shirts, and white
heavy cotton underwear. Two suits of evening dress tails,
one dinner jacket, one morning suit. The five pairs of shoes
on the shoe rack were all black. No light coloured walking
suits, no riding habits, no brown brogue walking shoes, no
scarfs or mufflers, windcheaters or climbing anoraks, nothing
that had either colour or pattern or had been bought with
frivolous intent. The bathroom contained no aftershave lo-
tions, but plenty of toothpaste, mouthwash, and a gross of
Bisodol tablets.

Aveyard met Bruton in the small kitchenette. "Find anything, Jim?" he said.

Jim shook his head. "Nothing I didn't expect," he said, "except that he was a compulsive eater." He pointed to the cupboard, in the lock of which was a key. He opened the cupboard using the end of a pencil. Inside the cupboard were two boxes of tins of frankfurter sausages, a box of jars of potato salad, and a box of Turkish Delight. "You can just see him, can't you," Bruton said, "having a good meal downstairs, scuttling back up here to make himself frankfurters and potato salad and read the *Financial Times*."

"Or *Burke's Peerage*. No wonder he needed the gross of Bisodol tablets," Aveyard said. It was in keeping with the opinion Aveyard had formed of Rupert Samuel from what Arthur Porter had told him, and what he had found. Many people are compulsive eaters, especially when they have no other emotional outlet. Aveyard himself was a gourmet cook, self-taught. He knew how much cooking a meal to be eaten in convivial company could relax him and widen his thoughts. Rupert Samuel's mind, firmly fixed along the route of moneymaking and his family title, would admit no such frivolity, but his body would crave an outlet and this he would find stuffing himself with convenience foods.

Aveyard walked across and stood at the door of the apartment looking back over the scene, Jim Bruton silent beside him. Then Aveyard went to examine the blood stains John Victor had pointed out. Though they were covered with the clear plastic he could imagine the arc along which they had fallen. "There's nothing here for us," he said. "Let the forensic boys come back when they've had their tea and finish off. It'll be up to John Victor to find whatever he can, but I don't hold out much hope. We'll solve this one by finding the motive, not by forensics. It's too simple for a forensic job. Man walks into the room bringing the sword with him, stands in front of Rupert Samuel and brings the sword down on his neck. One of the two things we can say, I suppose, is that he knew Rupert Samuel and Rupert Samuel knew him. And it can't have been the butler, because he's too short."

"You're not going to give me a routine about it being a left-handed Cantonese Chinaman, who bought his tobacco off the East India Wharf, are you?" Bruton asked, smiling.

"You'll be lucky," Aveyard said. "That went out with Conan Doyle."

CHAPTER SEVEN

The landrover came slowly down the lane, its lights out. The driver inched his way forward through the blackness, using the lighter earth of the tracks as his only guide. The night was still thick with no sign of a moon. He heard a rustle from the older man beside him.

"You're not going to light a bloody cigarette?"

The old man laughed nervously. "I forgot for the moment."

"Well, don't bloody forget. Honestly, Tom, sometimes I think I need my head examining, bringing you out with me."

"No need to get bloody huffy."

They drew near the end of the lane. "He should be here somewhere," the driver said, "so keep your eyes open. We don't want to run into a bloody copper."

"I liked it a lot better when I was doing country houses for the silver!" Tom said. "Time to take it easy on them jobs, draw the curtains, smoke a cigarette, take a drink of the whisky. Look at me now, riding the bloody range. And if there's one thing I can't stand it's Zane bloody Grey and his Wild West adventures."

A figure materialized out of the shadow beneath a tree at the end of the lane. A cigarette lighter flared briefly and was quickly extinguished.

"That's it," the driver said, "it's all clear." He turned the car out of the lane and onto the road, hearing the squeak of the gate as it was drawn shut behind them. The figure came and stood beside the cab of the landrover.

"All right, Fred?" he said.

"Roger, David." Fred reached inside the pocket of his ex-army parka. "Sweet as a nut." He took out a roll of notes and handed them to David. "I think you'll find fifty quid there, all good ones. Tom made them hisself this morning."

"He'd better not have," David said, "I don't want any bent stuff."

"Bent stuff! Tom came out of that game years ago. No money in it."

"I've found a good one for you tomorrow," David said. "I've drawn it on a map as usual. It's a doddle. You could pick up three if you're quick."

"That means the Bedford. I'm not sure they've got the winch mended."

"That's your business, not mine."

"Don't get bloody shirty, not with me, mate."

"I'm not, but I go through all this business lining them up and you start talking to me about winches."

"Tom here will fix it. He's still got his bottles left over from last year. It'll be a change, mending instead of cutting, won't it, Tom?"

Tom grunted. "Are we going to piss off home or sit here blabbering all night?"

"Right. See you tomorrow," Fred said, as he tucked the map into his inside pocket, let in the gear and drove away.

Paul Krancek was taken prisoner by the soldiers of the 9th Australian Division in the battle of Alam Halfa on 31 August 1942 and there ended an inauspicious military career that like so many others had only begun as a result of excessive drinking. Early in 1939 Paul Krancek and two of his poet friends decided after a night on the town that there was no point in subsisting at poverty level when the German Army just across the border was willing to pay good money to any-one embracing the Nazi philosophy. Truth to tell, when he enlisted Paul Krancek was not in a condition to spell the word Nazi. He was attached to an Infantry Regiment but it quickly became apparent that this dreamy poetic person was incapable of even the smallest act of militarism. However, the army had much need of supporting arms and a broom was thrust into Krancek's hand instead of a rifle and bayonet.

Paul Krancek, figuratively speaking, pushed his broom all the way across Germany and most of the face of North Africa. At the time of his capture he was sweeping out the camp Officers' Mess from which his warlike superiors had gone to battle leaving behind the remnants of a black bread, liverwurst and cheese breakfast. When he eventually reached prisoner-of-war camp in England he thought himself in paradise when he was made librarian of the camp choir's music. Soon the regulations were relaxed somewhat and he was permitted to leave the camp under escort with the working parties who were employed on farms. His favourite assignment was to Bushden Hall in Northamptonshire, only ten miles from the prisoner-of-war camp in the grounds of the Duke of Buccleugh just outside Kettering. The butler took kindly to him and though on the records of the working assignment he was listed as a farm labourer, he spent his days in those servantless war years helping the butler maintain Bushden Hall in a state of something like cleanliness. Once again he took to the broom and there found contentment.

A number of Land Army girls were employed on the Bushden farms and Lord Bushden, absent on duties with the Royal Artillery, had given permission for a play-reading group to meet in the library. Among those who regularly attended were Paul Krancek, whose English was improving every day, and May Carter, who had a conscientious objection to serving with the A.T.S. It was inevitable that the dreamy poetic romantic German/Pole with his delicate sensitive face and his accent which sounded like a cross between Anton Walbrook and Charles Boyer, with his obvious hatred of war and violence, and his love of the delicate son-

nets of Keats and Shelley which thronged the library walls
of Bushden Hall in a plentiful abundance and to which she
introduced him, should win her heart.

When the hostilities in Europe ended and their two coun-
tries were no longer officially at war, Paul Krancek proposed
marriage to May Carter and was accepted. The commanding officer of the prisoner-of-war camp gave his blessing,
Lord Bushden, thanks to the intervention of his butler,
rented them a cottage in Ice Tower Lane, and when the
prisoners were released from the camp and allowed to select
their country of repatriation, Paul and May settled down in
Bushden to connubial bliss. Paul was given employment as
"inside" gardener and spent his time tending the plants in
Lord Bushden's extensive greenhouses and Orangeries. May
worked for a while as assistant tutor to the two Bushden
boys, but ill health overtook her and she was obliged to give
up that employment.

In 1952 May recovered in health and even contemplated
going back to work until she found herself pregnant. Paul
and she were overjoyed and a daughter was born and chris-
tened Matushka in memory of Paul's mother whom May had
never seen. May herself did not survive the birth. Paul
grieved for her but the village women were most helpful
and a succession of them came to the cottage and helped
him rear the child which he stubbornly refused to entrust to
the care of foster parents. The child grew strong and
healthy, and closely resembled her mother who, though not
beautiful, had an interesting friendly face and manner.

Paul Krancek missed his wife of course. He missed her
conversation, he missed her reading out loud to him from
some book in her hand, saying, "Oh Paul, you must listen to
this, you must hear how beautiful this is." She had opened
up for him a whole world of English reading and music;
they'd been prominent members of the Bushden Choral Society led by William Tew and all the Tew family, with
Thomas Dalgleish taking off his dog collar to play the piano

and organ and Roger Bowman who ran the mobile village
shop and Fred Latham and all his family who ran the other,
static shop in Leather Lane on the edge of the Green. Somehow after May died Paul could not bring himself to continue
these choral activities without her and he retired more and
more into himself and his Polish ancestry.

What started him off with the discovery in the Northampton market of some Polish papers on a second-hand book
stall. They had once been a book but the binding had come
apart and the back page had long since been lost. The title
could be translated as "The Memoirs of a Polish Countess."
One by one he discovered other Polish papers in other street
markets. Scraps of old Polish music, genealogies of old
Polish families, some of them even with details of old Polish
castles and houses. Over the years his passionate hobby
became the collection of old Polish printing; anything in
Polish on paper interested him enormously. Once he returned from Oundle in a great state of excitement and pored
over a document he had purchased very cheaply. For several
days he hugged the passionate thought to himself that what
he had uncovered was an original letter from Frédéric Cho-
pin, containing—wonder upon wonders—a few staves of music jotted down to emphasize a point. An expert from the
British Museum, however, to whom he hastened to show the
paper, dashed his hopes. But the stiff crackling scrap,
mounted behind glass, became his prized possession. In his
heart he never really believed the expert from the British
Museum.

One section of his filing cabinets was devoted entirely to
early Polish songs and he had the complete works of Weczakowsky in a volume that had cost him two pounds in the
market in Leeds, to which town many Polish Jewish refu-
gees had fled during the early 1930s. One day Paul Krancek
showed his collection to Roger Bowman and together they
hummed and sang and played on Krancek's battered piano
many of the old Polish melodies. It was a wonderful evening

together and Paul hoped that he and Roger Bowman, who was thirty-five and unmarried, might strike a deeper friendship since they both obviously shared the same interests.

One evening he heard that the choir was rehearsing a new anthem which Roger Bowman had composed. Apparently the music had been sent to the B.B.C. in Birmingham and they were going to come down and record it. The whole village was agog. Fancy one of them doing a broadcast on the B.B.C. Roger Bowman himself was going to play the organ and everybody in the choir was going to sing. The vicar, though displaced as organist on this occasion, was very magnanimous and said that even though the work was of a secular nature he would ask Lord Bushden's consent for the performance to be recorded in the church itself, whose fine acoustic was well known.

The recording took place one Thursday evening and the entire village came to the church to hear the choir perform. After such a long absence Paul Krancek did not feel he could take a place in the choir, but he slipped into the church just before the recording began and sat unseen by the baptismal font. The B.B.C. recording engineer had adjusted his microphones. The van was parked in the churchyard with its tape-recording machine. The recording engineer gave the cue, the vicar raised his baton and on a nod from the engineer the baton came down and the first melodious tones of the organ were heard playing the introduction. Sixteen bars later the choir began to sing, and Paul Krancek felt a wistful sadness in himself that his voice was not among those soaring to the roof of the church.

His wistful sadness however quickly turned to a deep inner rage when he recognized in the anthem the work of Weczakowsky that he and Roger Bowman had sung together in such a spirit of friendship only a short time ago. When the recording was finished he slipped from the church and hurried back to his cottage. He reached for the book of Weczakowsky's music. Two pages had been brutally torn from it.

CHAPTER EIGHT

While Jim Bruton helped Inspector Roberts to set up the incidents room, Bill Aveyard walked back to the pub with Amanda Tew. The time was 9 o'clock. Now the stars had come out and shone brightly over the streets of Bushden and a quarter moon was visible over the fields of Home Farm. They walked together down Hall Way, both obviously thinking about the missing man.

"I'll pack a few things," she said, "and move into the Hall. There's a room at the back near the kennels that they've always let me use whenever I've wanted. I'll be nearer there when you find him."

"He could be a long way away," Aveyard said, glancing at her.

She shook her head. "He won't go far. He's never been away from home except to go to various places when he was a very young boy for medical examinations. He always hated being away from home and the village. Lord and Lady Bushden have never been away together all the time I've known him. Always one of them would stay here. About five years ago they tried to take him to Bournemouth for a holiday, but the minute the car left the village he started shouting and they turned around and came back. They never tried again. They were both absolutely devoted to him. You know Lord Bushden was going to let him have the title? Everybody realized that would be the end of it because David Arthur could never get married and the Bushden line would die out. I think apart from anything else, nobody in the village wanted to see the title go to Rupert

Samuel. Now we're outside the house I don't mind telling you everybody hated him. Even as a boy he was a mean, sadistic, vicious little bastard. Of course, he would inherit all the money, but the villagers don't think about things like that. It's who's going to be the Lord of the Manor that counts."

They had reached the door of the pub. "I'll wait while you pack your bag," Bill Aveyard said, "and walk back with you." Amanda Tew was a pleasant girl to be with. Aveyard could well understand why she and David Arthur had been such good friends. While she went through to the living quarters at the back of the pub he went into the saloon bar and ordered a half pint of beer.

"Bottled beer all right?" William Tew said. "I'm changing the brewery and the new draught hasn't settled yet, but I've got a bottle of Rudkins, if that's any good to you."

"That's my sort of beer," Aveyard said.

"Better than this tasteless muck the big boys spew out," William Tew said with a laugh. "You'll be the policeman old Porter mentioned."

"Don't tell me how young I look."

"I wasn't going to. Horses for courses, that's my motto. If you're no good they'd give you the bullet, wouldn't they?"

Aveyard laughed. "I suppose so. Will you have one?" William Tew poured himself a glass of bottled beer and stood at the counter drinking. Only three men were sitting in the saloon bar. Aveyard looked slowly around. They were eyeing him. "Evening," each one said in turn. Aveyard knew Bruton would have all their names before the evening was out and restricted himself to saying "Good evening," back.

"Aught you can tell us?" William asked, blunt and direct as usual.

"Not a lot as yet," Aveyard said.

"They tell me as two have died," William said, and Aveyard confirmed it with a nod of his head.

"I'm not surprised," William said. "Breaks your heart. One bad apple and the whole barrel goes off."

"David Arthur?"

"Not on your life. Good as gold, that lad. Some say he was simple, but I'll never believe it. His brother held him back. Look," William Tew said, "that David Arthur, supposed to be simple, and yet many a man who comes regularly into this pub can't beat him at cribbage, and for that game you need a head on your shoulders."

He looked towards the man sitting at a table by the door, a man of about thirty. "Bill," he said, "tell the superintendent here about the time you and David Arthur made that great firework when you were lads together, like one of them Congreves they used for mortars in the old days. The two of 'em concocted it out of a handful of rockets they bought from Latham's shop for bonfire night and they filled it with shotgun charges and some stuff they made out of weedkiller and sugar or something. When that lot went up in the air and exploded it practically flattened the village. Nothing wrong with that lad, if you ask me. He used to turn out regular for the cricket club, and what he couldn't do with a cricket bat in his hands, boundaries and sneak 'em through the slips with a late cut. Trouble was, if he'd been born of humble parents he'd have spent his life working a farm and nobody would have been any wiser. But he is to be a Lord, isn't he, and Lords have to be better than the rest of us and they pushed him on. What with the pushing and that rotten brother of his he went in on himself, if you know what I mean. Best thing they could have done would have been to give him a cottage in the village and let him come in this pub every night. Him and my Amanda could have made a go of it, just the two of them, left alone to make their own lives. Aye, God moves in His mysterious ways."

At that moment Amanda came through from the private quarters into the saloon bar. "I'm going to make my bed up there, Dad," she said, "until they find him."

"Yes, I reckon that's the best place for you, lass," William Tew said as he kissed her good night on the cheek.

Bill Aveyard and Amanda Tew came out of the pub, on Leather Lane. The Green was in front of them. "Would you mind if we went the long way back?" Aveyard said.

She laughed. "The slow boat to China . . . ?"

"Any other time. Right now I'd like a guided tour of the village if you don't mind."

"Why not, it's a pleasant evening and it'll help take my thoughts off David Arthur."

They turned left down Priest's Way towards the church. "All this part of the world was very active during the time of the Reformation," she said. "All the big houses contain Priests' Holes. You know about the one in Bushden Hall, of course, but there are several others. Religious intolerance seems so unbelievable in this day and age, doesn't it?"

"Until you remember Israel, and South America."

They turned right into Ice Tower Lane, and Amanda Tew named the tenant of each cottage they passed. "That's the Smiths', and that's the Robinsons', and that's the Kranceks', and that's the Battersbys' . . ." But Aveyard told her not to bother.

"It's not names I'm after," he said, "as much as general impressions."

At the end of Ice Tower Lane they came to a T-junction with Nether Way South, and turned right to go back up into the village. Amanda talked easily to him about life in the village, about the cohesion of a small settlement which had not been carved in two by a main road as had so many villages. Slowly a picture emerged of the dominance of the Hall, and the people who lived in it. Aveyard was surprised that in this modern age people could still accept an almost feudal tradition.

"That's the beauty of it," she said. "While it may seem feudal, it's actually benevolent."

"But, for example, you've told me that nobody can buy their own house here in the village. Lord Bushden will never sell."

"That's all a part of the tradition. Of course, when some of the young lads have grown up, and found themselves a wife outside the village, they've thought about buying a modern semi somewhere, but they are the type who'd leave the village anyway. For every one who goes, twenty want to come. When Old Agnes died last year, do you know the Estate Office had over fifty applications to rent the cottage from all over the county. The lad who took it, Willie Harkness, left the village five years ago to buy a semi at Wollaston and didn't like it. Now he's sold his semi, bought a business in Birton, and come back to live in Bushden."

They had reached a junction of roads on the side of the Green. Across the grass he could see the illuminated sign of the pub. "This is what we call Five Ends," she said, "and many people think it's because five roads end here, but that's our village joke. Five Catholics were hanged here, where the gibbet used to be, and the Five Ends are five deaths, remembered to this day. Every youngster in this village could tell you the names of the five who died here, even though they may not be able to remember Kings of England."

A small lorry was approaching slowly down North Nether Way. It stopped outside the gate of North End Farm. "That man could probably tell you all about the people of this village and the surrounding district," she said. "Roger Bowman. He runs the mobile shop. He's got everything on his cart, from sewing cottons to pounds of sugar. Goes round all the time, in the evenings as well, when there's no choir practice."

"Local man?"

"Priest's Way, back of the pub. Parks his van behind the pub, usually."

"What does your local shop feel about him taking the trade?"

"You have a suspicious mind, Superintendent. Fred Latham is a lazy blighter; he's pleased to lose all the business Roger Bowman gets. The two of them are a pair anyway; all they think about is the choir. That's all they can talk about since they did a broadcast over the B.B.C. Roger Bowman's own music, too, with the composer himself sitting at the organ. My, what a night that was. My dad sold out of beer for the first time in his life, had to send to Birton for extra bottles. And they drank him out of whisky, and rum. Lord Bushden gave the choir a gift of a pound a man to buy the first drink. He came to the pub himself to start them going. That's the sort of man he was," she said.

Aveyard looked quickly at her. There were tears in her eyes but she brushed them away. Now they were level with the mobile shop and Aveyard saw a man come out of the farm gate, carrying a folkweave basket in which were several Swiss rolls and cakes, obviously taken up to the farm door to tempt a customer. The man greeted Amanda, looked curiously at the superintendent. Amanda introduced them, but Bowman didn't immediately ask what Aveyard was doing there, to Aveyard's relief.

"I hear you're a composer?" Aveyard said.

"I have done a bit. Matter of fact, I had one on the B.B.C. quite recently. Went down well, they tell me," Bowman said deferentially. Aveyard smiled to himself. He knew the type. Big-headed smug bastard, he thought.

"You must be very proud."

"Well, it wasn't all my own work, you know," Bowman said with a late modesty. "Having such a good choir helped enormously."

"Miss Tew tells me you probably know as much as anybody what goes on around this district."

"Oh yes, official business, is it?"

"I'm afraid so."

"Well, I do see a lot. What sort of thing are you looking for?"

"You haven't seen David Arthur anywhere this evening, have you?" Amanda Tew burst out, unable to contain herself longer. Roger Bowman looked at her, then back at Aveyard. "I *never* see Mr. David Arthur anywhere on *my* rounds," he said. "You know he never leaves the village." His face had shut tight as if expecting some kind of rebuttal, as if the question itself had been a trap.

"No, I know that, but I just wondered . . . ?"

"Just wondered what, Amanda . . . ?"

"Miss Tew's a bit upset," Aveyard said. "We can't find David Arthur Bushden, that's all."

"And might a body ask why you're looking for him?"

Aveyard noted the waspish way Bowman spoke and felt the hair curl at the back of his neck. One sort of man always turned Aveyard off, and Roger Bowman was that sort, of that he was convinced. Still, it was all legal now, wasn't it?

"I'm afraid I shall have to call that an official secret," Aveyard said, deliberately pompous, and took Amanda Tew's arm and started her walking up the street.

"Well, good night," Roger Bowman called after them but Aveyard couldn't bring himself to utter anything other than a muttered "Goodbye."

A police car was standing at the top of North Nether Way, where the High Street makes a T-junction. Aveyard walked across to the car with Amanda. The constable driver leaped out when he saw the superintendent approach. He smelled of tobacco when he spoke. "Inspector Roberts has placed us here, Sir, on general watch."

"Then you ought to be parked *off* the road," Aveyard said, "not *on* it where everybody can see you." He immediately regretted his bad temper; somehow the brief encounter with Bowman had put him out of sorts.

"Yes, Superintendent."

"You've got a description of the man we're looking for?"

"Yes, Superintendent."

"That's the man I want you to watch out for most particularly. The description says he's a bit simple, but a few things I've heard make me believe he might have a head on his shoulders. If he sees you . . ."

"He might scarper the other way . . ."

"That's right." Aveyard turned to go, suddenly heard the radio squawk in the car. He put his head in through the window.

"Very good, Able Baker Fox," the voice was saying, "we've notified all departments."

The constable in the car tried to sit upright as he pressed the button of the microphone. "Able Baker Fox, Roger and out," he said.

Aveyard withdrew his head. "What was all that about?" he asked the constable driver.

"Funny thing," the driver said. "When I was sitting here, I suddenly saw a face I recognized. Hadn't seen it for a year or two, when I was driving in Birmingham. Before I got my posting here."

"Who was it?"

"A lad we used to call Birmingham Fred. He was sent down a time or two for Grievous Bodily Harm. A right tearaway. I heard that last time he came out, he went straight. Opened a shop or something. Anyway, here he was tonight, driving past me in a landrover, large as life. And sitting next to him was an old peterman, Tom Phillips. Used to specialize in country-house silver. So I thought I'd better pass the word around that they were in the district. Just in case they were up to their old tricks."

"Good man," Aveyard said. "That's what I like to see, a man who stays awake at the wheel when he's on watch, and then uses his initiative. When you get back in tonight, tell the sergeant I said to put you on the report. I'll work out the wording myself, tomorrow."

"That's very kind of you, Sir," the driver said, smiling with pleasure.

"Now get that car out of sight," Aveyard said, "or I'll have you on the report for a different reason."

The driver saluted him and leaped back into the car, which he drove smoothly into the deeper darkness beneath a tree by the side of the road.

Bill Aveyard and Amanda Tew continued their walk back to the Hall. Both were silent, all the way.

CHAPTER NINE

When Aveyard arrived back at Bushden Hall, the bodies of Lord Bushden and his son, Rupert Samuel, had both been removed to the forensic laboratory in Birton. Inspector Bradbury had gone with them as certifying officer. His would be the unpleasant task of watching everything John Victor did, countersigning every label John Victor would place on each specimen, so that, if the matter came to court and forensic testimony were given, he could swear to the authenticity of the source of the evidence.

John Victor had left a message with Inspector Roberts in the Incidents Room, asking Aveyard to call him. The message was numbered and timed, as would be every single communication received in that room. Aveyard looked about the large dining hall, its high walls hung with heraldic shields, the armorial insignia of the Bushden family going down through the ages back to the days of William the Conqueror, when a Knight had been awarded a grant of land for his bravery on the field. The actual title Lord Bushden of Bushden had been awarded by King Henry II, and the building of the Hall and its surrounding village dated from that time.

Aveyard's own desk was the dining-room table, over twenty feet long and three inches thick, made from a single plank of wood, its edge inlaid with a thin strip of brass. His chair was the chair Lord Bushden traditionally used, high, with lion's head arms, and a carved back over a leather padded rest and seat. "I shan't be using that," Aveyard said when he looked at it.

Bruton had been smiling. "I told the lads you wouldn't," he said, "but they thought you ought to try it on, see how it fits."

Aveyard snorted. He had no delusions of grandeur. "That's a chair was built for the arse of a Lord, not mine," he said. He noticed that his accustomed chair had been brought with the other paraphernalia of filing cabinets and copying machines, typewriters and staplers and pencil sharpers. Bruton pulled the carver away, and put Aveyard's comfortable wooden chair with its moquette seat in its place.

"I'll talk to John Victor first," Aveyard said.

They quickly connected the telephone exchange they'd already installed on the direct line to the police laboratory, and John Victor himself picked up the phone on the other end.

"First tests on Lord Bushden show natural causes," John Victor said. "Dr. Samson's here, and we're in consultation."

"If that means he's trying to dissuade you from opening the head to look at that tumour . . ." Aveyard said.

"I think I know my responsibility, Superintendent."

"Good." Aveyard could almost hear again Samson's "cheeky young whippersnapper," but didn't care. Damn their medical ethic. The murder of Rupert Samuel didn't take away the fact that Lord Bushden had asked for the police, and he wanted a complete autopsy.

"Now, about the other one, the son. Everything so far is consistent with what we can see, a blow from a sharp instrument which severed the jugular vein and caused extensive loss of blood, etc. I presume that at this stage you don't want a lot of medical information—I'll be putting it in my report anyway, but I can say I think the sword killed him."

"And we can act on that supposition?"

"For the time being."

This was one of the reasons Aveyard liked working with John Victor. He was one of the few pathologists prepared to speculate, once he had sure ground on which that speculation could be based. The other pathologists tended to surround themselves with "ifs" and "buts" and medical obscurity. John Victor knew enough about investigations to realize that the police, in the early stages, needed the pathologist to start them off in the right direction; the detailed work, the close co-operation between Science and the Law could come later. John Victor also knew Aveyard would never hold him to a speculation, never say later, if the first "informed" guess proved wrong, that the pathologist had misled him. No murder is ever quite what it seems at first sight, and both were aware of that.

"I have something you might be able to start on," John Victor said. "I found some fibres. By the spot where I estimate the murderer must have stood."

"You mean the assailant . . ."

"You're quite right, Superintendent. The assailant. These fibres, they're vegetable, brownish red, probably off a flower but as yet I can't tell you which."

"I'm grateful enough for that at this stage."

"Unless I have a lucky fluke and somebody happens to recognize it, it may take a time to identify which flower."

"What's so strange about vegetable fibres? This is a country home, people walking in and out, bits of plants on their shoes."

"Ah yes, Superintendent, but I think you'll find when you look at the rest of the carpet it had been cleaned by a vacuum cleaner, within a short time of the attack."

"Before?"

"Even, possibly, after."

A silence hung on the telephone. Aveyard could almost hear the smugness in John Victor's voice.

"What do you mean, 'possibly after?'" he said quietly. Those who knew him had learned to listen to that cold deliberate voice.

"I took an oblique shot of the pile of that carpet," John Victor said. "Turned out very well. Some of the footprints of what I can only assume is the assailant have been vacuum cleaned away."

Aveyard put down the telephone. His face was grim.

"I want to speak to Porter," he said to Jim Bruton, who'd taken a seat at the long table near him, "and I don't want to waste a lot of time about it."

Bruton got up from the table and went quickly out of the dining room.

The pile on a good carpet stands upright, and viewed from the side, under magnification, each strand can be seen, tall and erect as a forest tree. The weight of a foot, however, will bend the fibres down and often a long time elapses before natural springiness reasserts itself and the fibres come upright again. When a carpet is vacuum cleaned, the piles are sucked upright immediately. Under oblique photography, and subsequent enlargement, a good carpet will clearly reveal the presence of footprints. Aveyard and John Victor had been relying on that.

When Arthur Porter came in, he'd been subjected to the softening up process of which Bruton was a master. "I don't know why the superintendent seems so angry. What could you have been doing? The super's a Holy Terror when he gets going. One thing I must say, though, he's a fair man and very understanding to people who cooperate with him, tell him all they know," etc., etc.

"After the discovery of Mr. Rupert Samuel's body, did you vacuum clean the carpet?" Aveyard asked, quietly.

Arthur Porter looked round as if trapped. No one else was looking at him except the superintendent. Even Bruton appeared to be scribbling purposefully on a sheet of paper but Aveyard knew he was ready to take down in shorthand everything Porter might say.

"I might have done," Porter said, "but the sight of that body was so shocking, I don't remember. I don't remember."

Feigned amnesia is easy to cope with, but can often take time in an investigation.

"Come on, Porter, you know you *can* remember if you want to," Aveyard said, his voice still quiet. "Think of what Lady Bushden would say if we had to arrest you and take you down to headquarters in a police car and lock you up with a lot of common criminals until you *could* remember?"

It worked like a charm. "Yes," Arthur Porter said, almost whispering, "I cleaned the carpet."

"Why?"

"Because there was something on it. It's so very difficult these days, Superintendent."

"What's difficult, Porter?"

"Servants, Superintendent, they are the bane of my existence. The young people don't seem to care any more. I have the greatest difficulty . . ."

Aveyard waited patiently. Porter would tell him what he wanted to know, but in his own way, his own time.

"Tell me about the carpet . . ."

"It began this afternoon. I'd told the staff they could take the evening off. I'd even arranged matters so they could leave a little earlier than usual. Matushka Krancek works in the house, you know, like her father and mother before her. She looks after Mr. Rupert Samuel's rooms and Mr. David Arthur's. Lady Bushden went up to Mr. Rupert Samuel's rooms, early this evening, must have been about five o'clock, and the room had not been cleaned properly. The carpet had not even been vacuumed. I had to speak rather sharply to Matushka and send her back up there. Mr. Rupert Samuel is so particular you see, and would create most terribly if his rooms were not done properly; Lady Bushden knew this, and no doubt wanted to avoid a scene when she insisted the carpet be done again. You understand, Superintendent, she didn't insist, but I knew her well enough to read the storm signals."

"So the carpet was vacuum cleaned late this afternoon?"

"That is correct."

"And you cleaned it again . . . ?"

"Yes." Porter bowed his head in sorrow. "I know now it was wrong. I've probably brushed away a number of—what do you call them—clues . . . ?"

"Don't worry about what we call them; that's not important. Tell me exactly when, and why, you cleaned the carpet."

Now Porter looked at him again, and a hint of defiance had come into his manner. "I did it for the best of reasons," he said, "but I cannot expect you to understand that. When I saw Mr. Rupert Samuel lying on the carpet, my first thoughts were for her Ladyship. I knew how much the sight would distress her, having just lost her husband. I wanted only to protect her, so far as it lay within my power. There was a quantity of a sort of grass near Mr. Rupert Samuel's body. I knew the sight of that would add to her pain, the thought that her son was lying on an unclean carpet in his final moments. So, I took the cleaner from where it is kept in the closet in Mr. Rupert Samuel's kitchen, and tidied up the carpet so that Lady Bushden would not see it."

Aveyard glanced at Bruton. Was such a thing conceivable in this day and age? When every television programme, every detective story, says quite clearly that nothing must be touched at the scene of a crime? Porter must have known what he was doing. "You *must* have known what you were doing," he said. Jim Bruton had raised his eyebrows, but Aveyard was in no mood to read the signal.

"Yes, Superintendent, I knew what I was doing," Porter said proudly. "I was protecting my Mistress from unnecessary pain. Throughout my life, that has always been one of the tasks I have honoured most highly."

Bruton coughed. Bruton never had a cough. "What is it, Jim?" Bill Aveyard said.

"Could I go and get the vacuum cleaner?"

Aveyard cursed himself for having let his amazement at

this old man interfere with his police thinking. That vacuum cleaner ought already to have been on its way to John Victor.

"Yes," he said, "and send it to John Victor fast as you can."

Bruton had already signalled to a constable further down the table who slid along, his pencil poised ready to take over the task of shorthand writer.

Aveyard looked at Porter.

"Did you do anything else you haven't told me about?" he asked.

Porter shook his head. "No, nothing," he said. "I suppose you're going to arrest me now? Impeding a policeman in the execution of his duty."

Aveyard smiled. "So you do watch television," he said, but then he waved his hand. "No, I'm not going to arrest you," he said. "Each of us does his duty the way he sees it, and though you were wrong to do what you did, I don't blame you for it."

Porter looked at him with no trace of a smile. "If there's nothing further you require, Sir . . . ?"

"No, Porter, nothing further at the moment."

When Porter had threaded his dignified way through the crowded dining hall, Aveyard picked up the telephone. "I'm sending you a vacuum cleaner," he said when the connection to John Victor had been made. "I think you'll find its contents will help you identify that plant you were talking about. And you were right. The carpet was cleaned *after* the attack had taken place. Seems the butler wanted the scene of the crime all neat and tidy for her Ladyship to examine. And we think we have 'bull' in the police force, eh?"

CHAPTER TEN

The message about Birmingham Fred spread rapidly
through the Birton police force mobile units. Friday night's
a quiet night until the pubs turn out and the mobile cars
were all unoccupied, cruising around. Car six picked up a
sight of the landrover going into Birton, and reported it. Car
three happened to catch sight of it coming out of Birton at
the other end. Car five followed it along the road into
Northampton, reported in, and car fourteen, which happened to be near the railway bridge at the other end of the
town, pulled over and waited in case the landrover should
come that way. It did, round the ring road. Car fourteen
followed it out along the road that leads to the motorway.

The landrover was out of luck. One of its rear lights failed
near the turn off to Kislingbury. Car fourteen radioed back,
received orders to wait until nearer the motorway. When
they got there, two other cars pulled out and parked, blocking the road. In one of them was a dog and its handler. The
landrover was boxed in. The handler held the dog about
eight feet from the passenger door; Tom took one look and
stayed where he was.

The police found a dead cow in the back of the landrover.
It had been killed with a humane killer.

"Where'd you get it?" they asked.

"I've never seen it before," Birmingham Fred said. "It
must have crawled in the back of the rover and died, while
we were having a drink in a pub."

Even Tom didn't think that was a likely story, and wasn't
amused when the police driver, taking him back to Birton,

kept calling him "pardner" and singing "I'm a-heading fur the last round-up" in a Gene Autry voice.

Aveyard surveyed the room in which Lord Bushden's body had lain. The body had been removed, of course, to the police laboratory, the clothing Lord Bushden had worn sealed inside a plastic bag for detailed examination. Off the bedroom was a bathroom and two dressing rooms. One contained Lady Bushden's clothing, the other that of her husband. That's unusual, he thought. Usually at that level, lords and ladies maintain separate apartments, and sleeping together is something for the common folk. But then he remembered her sentence. "My husband was my entire life." Of course they would have lived and slept together.

Beyond the dressing rooms was a sitting room, which gave on to the upper landing. It was cosily furnished in vigorous chintz-covered comfortable furniture. On a side table were Scrabble, Mah Jongh, and a box of chess men. There was a pair of leather-bound books on the spine of which the word Jotto had been printed in gold. Lord and Lady Bushden had obviously spent many hours playing the word game together. In the recess formed by the window was a writing desk and on it two silver clips held invitation cards. "The Honourable Company of Leather Merchants invites . . . Your presence is humbly solicited . . ." On the top of the cabinet was a circular mount from which several rubber stamps were hanging. The bottom of the mount concealed an inking pad. Aveyard looked at the stamps. REFUSE, ACCEPT, ACCEPT FOR A FEE FOR CHARITY. The last one he looked at no doubt had a humorous intent. WILD HORSES WOULDN'T. He flipped through the cards in the clips. All had been stamped. Lord and Lady Bushden wouldn't attend the Annual Ball of the Chamber of Trade—wild horses wouldn't allow them to do so. Aveyard smiled. He'd been invited to that ghastly affair in the Birton Solarium often enough, but luckily duty had always given him a way out. Once or twice he'd had to volunteer to replace someone else to avoid going, but the extra duty had been worth it.

He saw that Lord and Lady Bushden had been intending to go to the Annual Police Ball. "Good for you," he said to himself. He'd also missed that particular function five years in a row, but not because he'd wanted to.

There was another writing table in the room. He opened it and saw correspondence addressed to Lord Bushden. This was obviously the sorting of a much larger bulk of letters, and contained only the personal ones. Fellow Conservatives asking Lord Bushden how he intended to vote on an issue in the House of Lords. A long plea from the Leader of the House about capital punishment. Was Bushden for or against? Would he care to make his opinions known "in certain quarters," wherever they may be. The right-hand drawer contained family correspondence. Several letters addressed to "Dad." Others addressed to "Father." Some, in a fine, almost classic script, simply said, "Willie."

The letters were stacked neatly, but one had been pushed hastily into the pile and was out of line with the others. It was also in the pile of letters addressed to "Father," though this envelope carried the name "Dad." For some reason, Aveyard instinctively reached for his handkerchief and held the letter by a corner. Then he used the paperknife from the bureau to draw the piece of paper out of the envelope. The message was undated, written in a broad round hand, with the letters carefully drawn in line, as if the writer had used a ruler to guide his hand; the paper was thick and embossed. On the top were the words "From David Arthur." There'd be other notepaper, no doubt the family crest. This was intended for informal family communications.

The message on the paper was very simple, though no one could call it simple-minded. "My dear Dad, I have been thinking about the title as you asked, and you have discussed its implications with me over a long period of time. I recognize that whoever holds it must bear a heavy burden of responsibility of which I do not believe myself to be capable. For too long I have acted the role of coward and simpleton and now find myself incapable of any other. Nothing so much becomes a man called to high responsibility as his manner of refusing it, and therefore, by the time you read this note, I shall have gone to join those other Lords and Ladies we have so often admired together. Your loving son, D.A."

Aveyard read the note again. He could not believe his eyes. This man, a simpleton? What utter, utter nonsense. He turned the page over carefully. Nothing was written on the back though the paper appeared to be stained slightly at the bottom. He pried the envelope open without touching it. At the bottom of it he was able to discern a few specks of what appeared to be seeds of some kind. He reached into his pocket, brought out the plastic bags he always carried on a murder investigation. It was a simple matter to put the sheet of notepaper into one bag, the envelope into another, seal each of them and carry them away with him. In the Incidents Room, he handed the bags to Inspector Roberts. "Label these for me," he said, "and have them taken right away to forensic."

"Can you tell me where they are from?"

"The top right-hand drawer of the writing bureau in Lord Bushden's sitting room. I'd like them tried for fingerprints, though with paper as thick as that, I doubt if you'll get anything."

Jim Bruton came into the Incidents Room. "I've got the house-to-house going," he said. He handed Aveyard a questionnaire. Aveyard read it. When a constable goes to a door, he carries a clipboard of roneoed forms. The top of the form contains a space for the name and address of the person questioned. The rest of the form carries a number of fixed questions, devised usually by the officer in charge of the investigation. Bruton had worked with Aveyard often enough to know what questions he'd like to see.

Aveyard handed it back. "I don't think it'll yield any-thing," he said, dispiritedly.

Bruton noticed his manner but said nothing. He took the Incidents Book from the table, read it to see if any of the messages concerned him. He noted the packet Aveyard had sent to forensic, but didn't ask what it was. Bill Aveyard would tell him when he wanted him to know.

"How long are you going to stay, Superintendent?" he asked.

Bill Aveyard looked at his watch. "Eleven o'clock?" he said incredulously. Bruton nodded. Aveyard looked about him. Two girl typists were transcribing the pencil written notes of the constables who'd already returned with the question-naires. They'd be at it until three in the morning. Roberts would read each typed note, sifting it for information, set-ting aside those he thought Aveyard ought to see. Soon the reports would start coming from forensic to be typed, dupli-cated and held for Aveyard's scrutiny. The door of the din-ing room opened, and Arthur Porter stood there, waiting. Bruton beckoned for him to come in. Porter walked to where the superintendent was seated.

"Her Ladyship sends her compliments, Sir, and wonders if you will require anything further of her this evening. If not, she's asked me to tell you she will be in the Blue Guest Room. I've connected the bell system so that, if you press the button on the wall, I shall hear it wherever I might be."

"Where might you be?" Inspector Roberts said, his pencil poised over his pad. Inspector Roberts wrote everything down, the best incidents officer on the Birton force.

"I shall be in my pantry," Porter said, with great dignity.

"And where is that, if I might make so bold?"

"The last door on the right, off the hall."

That fact was noted on the pad.

"I shall not be asleep," Porter added.

"None of us will be," Aveyard said gruffly.

When the butler had gone, he got up and stretched his

arms, relieving a crick in his shoulder blades. "Feel like a walk, Jim?" he asked. Jim Bruton got his overcoat from a side table, where it had been put with the superintendent's anorak.

"We'll be round the village," Aveyard said to Inspector Roberts, who glanced at his watch and wrote that down too. Bruton reached into his pocket, produced a walkie-talkie radio. "You can get us on this," he said, "code call A5."

Now the moon had risen and they could see the grounds of the Hall quite clearly. They walked towards the massive entrance gates that fronted on to the High Street. The gates were never closed. As they walked out, they met Amanda Tew, coming in.

"Would you believe it, I forgot my toothpaste," she said.

She stood nervously for a moment, wondering if they wanted to talk to her, but then she said good night and hastened up the drive. "That's funny," Bruton said. "I'd have thought she'd want to know if we'd found him."

That fact was filed in his mind. Together with the fact that she'd come up the High Street, when the shortest way from the pub would be Priest's Way.

"Are we going anywhere special, or just wandering?" he asked.

"Here we have a man who's supposed to be a simpleton," Aveyard said, "likes mechanical toys and so forth. Where would he be most likely to go in the village?"

Bruton didn't need to think. "The village shop. They always have little toys, these cars in plastic boxes, and sweets, and games . . ."

"Right. If there's a light still on, we'll tap on the door."

The light was still on; Fred Latham was restocking the shelves from boxes from the wholesaler. Aveyard tapped on the door. "I'm closed," Fred Latham shouted without turning round. He stacked the bars of chocolate in his hand on to the shelf then came across the shop and opened the door. "You'll have the police on me," he said, "selling stuff after closing hours . . ." But then he looked up and saw the two strangers. His hand reached instinctively to the edge of the door, and his face took on a determined look as he started to push the door shut.

"Police," Bruton said quickly. He saw the man relax. "Sergeant Bruton, and this is Superintendent Aveyard."

The man opened the door wider, and as they went in Bruton saw the wooden chair leg clipped to the side of the doorpost within easy reach. "That's a sensible precaution," he said, "but you should also have the door on a chain."

"You must be Fred Latham?" Aveyard said. He'd seen the electoral roll Bruton had produced earlier in the evening.

"That's me all right. I thought you were a couple of layabouts."

"Have you got a few minutes to spare, for a couple of layabouts?" Aveyard said, smiling, trying to put Latham at his ease.

Latham lifted the flap of the counter where it led to a door in the corner. "Come through to the back," he said. "I was finished here anyway. I like to stock up for Saturdays. Always one of my big days for bars of choc and cigs."

They went through into the back room. "Missis is in bed," he said. "She gets up early to take in the milk and the bread and pies." The room into which he led them was crammed with stock from floor to ceiling, boxes of tins and packets balanced crazily on every available surface but the table top. "We have another sitting room upstairs," he said, "and we retreat up there when the chaos gets too much for us." A kettle was singing quietly on a gas stove in the kitchenette. "Like a cup of tea or something alcoholic? Or there's coffee."

"Coffee would be fine," Aveyard said.

They sat round the table from which Fred Latham had cleared what were obviously invoices and bills, hanging them on clips on the side of the window frame. "The paperwork that goes into running a shop, you'd never believe. Mind you, from what they tell me, you have your share.

Your man was round with his questions, but I had to tell him I hadn't seen Mr. David Arthur. Not today, anyway. He was in yesterday and bought a few things."

"What sort of things?" Bruton asked quickly. Aveyard felt himself smiling. Bruton could never leave a fact in the air, must always pin it down.

"Oh, usual stuff. Packet of liquorice allsorts, bottle of ink —he liked that blue-black Parker Quink. I get it specially for him. A bag of sugar. One of the big jigsaws. He was a great one for the jigsaws. I got them specially for him too. He liked the really big ones, with a lot of pieces. I guess they helped him relax when he was a bit wound up."

"Was he often 'wound up'?" Aveyard asked quietly.

"It could vary so much with him. One day he'd come in, right as rain. The next day, well, he'd be giggling and have a funny look on his face and behave in a very childish manner. I had to tell him off a time or two, just like I would any other village lad, coming in here and larking about. Only this one was going on thirty and destined to be a Lord, if you see what I mean."

"How did he take to chastisement?" Aveyard asked.

"Well, very well. Never got clever with me, if you see what I mean. Never came the high hat. No, a word was all that was required. Somehow it seemed to remind him of his responsibilities."

"Let me ask you a straight question," Aveyard said.

"That means the answer is probably going to be embarrassing or compromising, or both . . ."

"No. I get the impression you knew him quite well."

"I suppose I knew him as well as anybody in this village, except Amanda Tew, of course."

"Right. Tell me, do *you* think he was simple-minded."

That thought had obviously not occurred to Fred Latham. He was silent for a moment or two, then he said, "How do you mean that? Do I think he was actually mentally sick, or was he just putting it on? Is that what you mean?"

"I suppose it is."

Again Fred was silent. "Hang on a minute," he said. He reached on a shelf behind him, dislodged a few packets of wrapping paper and from beneath them produced a book. He opened the book, flicking its pages to find the one he wanted. Then he spread the book on the table. "What do you think about that?" he asked. The page was covered in neat columns of figures, with entries down the left-hand side. Different types of stock. "The worst part of this business," Fred said, "is stock control. You never know how much of anything you've got left, since it's stacked a bit haywire. It's all right in the case of the non-perishables, but with the pies and the cakes, which last a few days but not for ever, you've got to watch yourself. Sell one bad pie . . . Or one stale cake . . ."

"And this is a stock control book?"

"Yes, just for the semi-perishables. This page was done for me by Mr. David Arthur. I couldn't do it as neatly, or as accurately, myself."

"So he wasn't simple?"

"That's what I'm trying to say. Not all the time. Sometimes he could be bright as a button, other times, well, I don't know. You know what they call schizophrenia? Well, I think he had it. Only he wasn't a Jekyll and Hyde. There was no evil in him that I ever saw. He was like, oh, how shall I put it, Morecambe and Wise, Abbott and Costello. One of them playing the wise man, the other one playing the fool and you never know which is which at any time."

Aveyard had registered the point. So had Bruton. "That helps me enormously," Aveyard said. "Can I ask you a couple of other questions? Who were his intimates in the village? Who did he know best, like most, dislike?"

"Well, that's a tough one. He knew everybody, everybody knew him. Not like his snotty-nosed brother who doesn't know anybody by name or face. Amanda Tew, of course, she was the Number One. They'd spent all their time together.

Paul Krancek, who works as inside gardener at the Hall, and always seemed to take to the lad, though Krancek's by way of being a thinking sort of a man. No, I can't put a finger on anybody he disliked. Oh yes, now I come to think of it, he didn't have much time for Roger Bowman of late. I don't know why that should be."

"How did his dislike show itself?" Bruton asked.

"Well, one day he surprised me by saying a man like that shouldn't be allowed in the village. When I asked him what he meant he got all cagey and said, "You'll see, you'll see." And then another time, Roger Bowman found a potato stuffed into his exhaust, and I knew who it was because David Arthur had just been in here and asked me for a potato and I told him to help himself out of the sack. I never gave it no mind until Bowman complained. But at the time, I just put it down to a childish prank. Let's face it, David Arthur hadn't even tried to hide what he was doing, just like a kid."

Just like a kid, Aveyard thought, as he and Bruton left Fred Latham and the shop, and walked back through the village towards the Hall. But kids don't wield sharp swords and chop people's jugular veins, do they, unless they have some kind of Jekyll and Hyde personality, and don't know what they were doing.

"Let's hope we find him soon, Jim," he said.

A massive search was proceeding, and the entire village was being combed—every barn, every outhouse, every garden shed, every inch of the Hall grounds. The mobile units patrolling the roads reported no sign of David Arthur, the house-to-house questioning revealed no trace.

Aveyard had just used the downstairs cloakroom the butler had put at their disposal and was walking back across the hall to the dining room when he saw a figure coming down the stairs. Lady Bushden was wearing a long housecoat buttoned to the throat, and comfortable slippers on her feet. She checked when she saw him. He stood at the bottom of the staircase, waiting for her. "I couldn't sleep, of course," she said.

"Didn't Dr. Samson leave you something?"

"He offered, but I didn't want it. I don't want to be unable to wake up if and when you find my son."

She walked across the hall to the door of the morning room.

"I keep a percolator in here," she said, "for when I don't wish to disturb Porter. He works so hard, poor dear man. Are you too busy to join me?"

"This is not yet my busy time," Aveyard said. "We're doing the routine things at the moment." He didn't tell her those "routine things" included an autopsy on her son and husband. She made his fifth cup of coffee of the evening.

"I've discovered a note," he said, "written I think by your son David Arthur to your husband. Your son didn't want the title, did you know."

"Yes, I do know. But my husband talked to him about it and, we hope, finally convinced him he must accept that responsibility. He seemed to do so." She had been sitting back in her chair with a completely relaxed air, but she got up and went to the windows. She drew aside the curtain sufficient to allow her to look out. The deep blue of her housecoat contrasted with the light oatmeal of the heavy curtains and Aveyard thought how well she looked standing there, how dignified, how "suitable." "Lords and Ladies?" Wasn't that the phrase David Arthur had used in his letter? "I go to join those Lords and Ladies . . ."

"How would he have managed?" Aveyard asked Lady Bushden, "without someone like you to help him as you must have helped your husband?"

She turned at the window. "How dark it is out there," she said absently. She was thinking of what he had said. "Well, of course, he couldn't have managed in the old days. Life was different then. So much to do, so many actual tasks to be

performed. But nowadays, you know, it's all quite different.
Many of them never even take their seat in the House any
more." She laughed nervously. "I find it such a bore," she
said, "when so many people take a title and then say, "it's
not going to make any difference to me. I'm just going to
live the life of an ordinary man." You can't live the life of an
ordinary man. Well, you couldn't. Now I'm not so sure.
David Arthur is a very *kindly* person, you know. He'd have
managed splendidly. I would have helped him, without in-
terfering, you understand . . ."

"To push potatoes up people's exhausts . . . ?"

She laughed. "Oh, you know about that do you? You must
have been talking to Mr. Latham. He was in such an awful
lather about it. 'If Mr. Bowman should ever find out,' he
said. Poor man was very worried. I talked to David Arthur
about it. He hadn't realized, you see, that Mr. Bowman
needs that vehicle to earn his living. There was no malice in
him."

"What would your son mean when he said to your husband in a letter, 'I go to join those other Lords and Ladies
we have so often admired together' . . . ?" Aveyard asked.

She came back across the room. "More coffee?" she asked,
but Aveyard refused.

"I've drunk too much already this evening," he said.

"What was that phrase? 'I go to join those other Lords and
Ladies we have so often admired together'?"

Aveyard nodded. Though Lady Bushden seemed to be a
little bit absent from their conversation, he knew she was
taking in every word. "I haven't the faintest idea," she said.
"It's rather odd, isn't it. Those *other* Lords and Ladies, admired together. Of course David Arthur and his father were
together a lot, and they read a lot—my husband always tried
to give David Arthur an education in something other than
reading, writing and 'rithmetic, you know. But *other* Lords
and Ladies . . . I can only suppose he was referring to something historical they'd read together, some Shakespeare play

perhaps, something that happened in a play perhaps. But nothing springs to mind."

Aveyard had mentioned the letter twice, now, but on neither occasion had Lady Bushden reacted to ask him, "which letter." Was it safe to assume she'd seen it, knew its contents?

Aveyard had read Shakespeare, of course, but nothing immediately came to his mind either. *Hamlet?* A play with a dominant brother in it? A simple son? He thought hard, but nothing came. *Lords and Ladies.* A curious phrase, anyway.

They both heard the knock at the door. Lady Bushden started. "That's probably for me," Aveyard said.

"Do you think they've found him . . . ?"

Aveyard went to the door. Bruton was standing outside. "The chief superintendent," he said, "on the telephone."

Aveyard excused himself and went out of the morning room, leaving Lady Bushden alone.

The chief was all business. "We've got a curious one, Bill," he said, "and there's just a remote chance it might have a connection for you. Can you spare the time to come in?"

"Give me five minutes."

The police car raced down the Birton Road at one mile an hour below the speed limit. "Have you heard, Superintendent?" the driver said, "they nobbled that man I was telling you about. Birmingham Fred. He had a dead cow in the back of that landrover. Fancy Birmingham Fred taking to cattle rustling in his old age."

"You must be feeling very happy," Aveyard said. "One of your tip-offs and an arrest already made."

Birmingham Fred was in the interview room. The chief came out when they told him the superintendent had arrived. "I wouldn't have called you in," he said, "but I understand the original word came from one of the cars on that job of yours. Since Fred was in your village . . ."

"It's worth finding out," Aveyard said. The chief had already received a telexed dossier on both Fred and Tom. The list of their convictions read like a Who's Who of crime. But neither had ever ventured into the open air before.

"Bit off your patch, weren't you, Fred?" Aveyard asked, opening the questioning in a friendly, informal way. The tough stuff could come later. For the moment, both were in the room together. Fred and Tom, Bill and his chief, and two shorthand writers, one taking down what Fred said, the other for Tom.

"You're a bit off, too, aren't you?" Fred said defiantly. "A super and a chief super. At this time of night. Don't you have any homes to go to? Put us down for the night. We'll still be here tomorrow." Fred needed time to think, didn't like this quick and concentrated attack before he'd had a chance to work something out.

"They've been cautioned, Chief?" Aveyard asked.

"Yes, but they know the book by heart."

"Incidentally, what brings you here?" Aveyard asked.

Though the two lags didn't know it, this was part of a technique Aveyard and his chief had worked out between themselves and practised many times. If it had a name it would be called, "Ignore the Prisoner." A man arrested and taken for questioning, especially a lag with as much form as these two, likes to feel himself the centre of attraction. It goes against the grain to be ignored. The chief smiled, recognizing Aveyard's overture.

"We've got so many men out," he said, "and I wanted to keep my hand in. Tackle something simple, you know."

"Well, there shouldn't be much difficulty tonight. Did you say the seed catalogue had arrived?"

"Yes, I've picked out a few things. By the way, I'm going to grow a few pot plants for that flat of yours. Like a barracks, your sitting room."

"What the bloody hell is this?" Fred demanded. "Bloody Gardening Club? Touch of the Percy Thrower's, that's what you two've got."

"Oh, I'm sorry, Fred," the chief said. "I'd forgotten you were here."

"Forgotten we was here, when your lads stopped us going home? By rights we ought to have been in kip by now."

"So you should."

"But you're not, are you?" Aveyard said, "and what's more I don't suppose you will be until you tell us what this is all about."

"Well, ask me some bloody questions, then."

One mad, one to go. Tom had said nothing, his eyes swivelling backwards and forwards like a man watching table tennis. "What are we going to do you for, Tom?" Aveyard said, "aiding and abetting, possession of, or what?"

"What about the Slaughter of Animals Act of '58?" the chief said. "That's a nasty one. They'll piss with laughing in Brum."

"You can't do me for that," Tom said, too quickly. Fred shot him a look of pure hatred.

"Keep it buttoned."

"Well, they can't."

The humane killer was on a side table, with a label tied round it. Aveyard walked over to it.

"I wouldn't know how to handle one of them things if you asked me," Tom said. "That was Fred's department."

Fred reared up in his seat but before he could move across to Tom the chief grabbed hold of his upper arm. The chief superintendent was a strong man, with hands like meat plates. "If you want it hard, Fred," he said, "just tell me. I'm used to your sort. Grievous Bodily Harm? I've squashed lads like you between my finger and thumb."

Aveyard walked behind Tom. "You prepared to make a statement?" Aveyard said. "Because if you're not, we may as well lock you both up in the same cell for the night . . ."

"I'll bloody murder him," Fred said.

"We know you will, but that doesn't bother us."

Tom looked up at Aveyard, twisting his head round to see

the superintendent. The chief beckoned to the shorthand writer, who went to the door. A sergeant came in. "Take Fred down," the chief said. The sergeant went back to the door.

"Wilkins and Peters," he said, "in here, quick." Two constables came in. "Right," the sergeant said, "on your feet, you."

Fred got to his feet. "I've got a name," he said.

"Not to me, you haven't," the sergeant said. "Now, left right left, fast as you like. We haven't got all night."

With the two constables beside him, Fred was virtually frog-marched from the room. It was a beautiful performance, designed to impress Tom as much as anything, to show him he couldn't win against the assembled might of the police force.

Aveyard sat down and reached inside the drawer of the desk. The chief sat down, but at the side table where Tom could not see him. Aveyard produced a packet of cigarettes from the drawer, and a box of matches. He opened the packet, slid a cigarette across the table. He struck a match on the side of the box and held out the flame. "You could get rid of all this very easy," Aveyard said. "Accessary. You didn't know what was going on. Fred asked you if you'd like a ride in his landrover, visit a couple of pubs, bit of a night out. You were dead surprised when he parked outside a field and produced a humane killer and slaughtered a cow. Of course, once he'd killed it, you were scared to call a copper. You knew he'd do you if you did. So you just, shall we say, went along with him, didn't you?"

Tom dragged on his cigarette, looking at Aveyard.

"An old hand like you," Aveyard said, "getting caught in a situation like that. Still, we understand how it can happen. You can't always pick your friends, can you?"

"But will the court understand?" Tom asked.

"That depends what evidence we offer, doesn't it? Nobody tells my chief what to say." Aveyard glanced across the room.

"That right, Chief, nobody tells you what evidence to offer?"

"That's right, Superintendent, and I'm a man who likes to show his gratitude in a practical way."

There it was, unstated but understood. You play ball with us, tell us all about it, and we'll only charge you with the minor offence of being an accessary. But the threat was implied. Hold out on us and we'll throw the book at you. Tom was an old lag. He knew the game. Aveyard was counting on that. He liked dealing with old lags. Some of them understood the Rules. Take a young old lag like Fred. He'd never admit to anything. Every inch of the case against him would have to be proved, would have to stand up in court. Hundreds of man hours would be wasted over the paper work alone. But an old old lag like Tom could save the force a lot of time and effort, and make life easy for himself at the same time. Aveyard had a fierce hatred of compromise and when he was an inspector, this often had impeded him. Now he was a superintendent, wiser if not much older, he was learning to bend with the wind. He still hated crime and criminals but recognized you had to fight according to rules they could understand, on ground they knew. Left hand scratches Right was a reality to men like Tom whose first question inevitably would be, what's in it for me?

"Do yourself a favour, Tom," Aveyard said.

"Accessary . . . ?"

"Accessary. No evidence offered . . ."

"Right," Tom said, "who takes it down?"

Aveyard beckoned to the shorthand writer. "Come here," he said, "where the gentleman can see you."

"The gentleman, eh?" Tom said, smiling, but the smile disappeared when Aveyard quickly said:

"Don't make me believe otherwise, Tom, because I can be a right bastard, when I'm riled."

"I'll bet you can, too. You young buggers are all the same."

Aveyard got up, and walked to the wall. Then he turned round and rested his fingertips against the wall, his body fully relaxed. "Right, Tom," he said, "let's have chapter and verse."

It was the same old story. Fred had met a man who knew a man who knew a man. The price of beef being what it was, cattle were suddenly worth pinching. Fred had gone straight after his last spell inside and had bought himself a butcher's shop. But Fred liked the high life, and you didn't get that out of the profits of a butcher's shop. Fred was bent, and when the chance came to get some of his raw materials free, he looked up Tom. Tom was getting old, and the country-house silver bit was played out anyway. Burglar alarms, and dogs, and anyway the silver wasn't worth much when they got it. Not like the old days. Cheap modern stuff that had to be melted down. A lot of EPNS bought for flash. Anyway, Tom was hard up. Fred was paying him £25 a trip. All he had to do was open gates and so on. Wind the winch. Some nights they took two cows, some nights two cows and a sheep or two. They used a lorry or the landrover, depending on what could be expected. That's what had happened tonight.

"How did you know where to find the beasts?" Aveyard asked.

"We got a tip. Fellow always gave us a map with two marks on it. One where we'd find the beasts, one where we'd find him to hand over the tip-off money."

"Who was the man?"

"I don't know."

"Come on, Tom. The deal was for a complete statement."

"Honest. I don't know. All I know was a figure used to appear in the dark, flash his lighter once to say everything was okay and there was no Law about. I never knew him. Never even saw his face proper."

"But you must know *something* about him?"

"Absolutely nothing. I never even saw his face. Every job, he was there afterwards. Gave us a map, took his lolly, and scarpered."

The chief was scribbling on a piece of paper. He went to the door and handed the paper to the duty sergeant waiting outside. Aveyard nodded his approval. If the chief hadn't done it, he would have. It didn't take the sergeant long to find the map in the pocket of the landrover. He put it in a brown paper envelope before he came back into the room and handed it to the chief. Aveyard noted it, nodded again. Tom, his statement finished, had a cunning look on his face.

"I did a job, about a month ago," he said. "Shoplifting in Bristol. You wouldn't like to forget all about this and send me down there? I'll cough to them in Bristol. They could even take this little lot into consideration."

Aveyard laughed out loud. "You're a cool one, Tom," he said. But there was an underlying note of seriousness in Tom's request. He didn't want to stand up in court alongside Fred. He didn't want Fred to know he'd coughed. He'd serve whatever he got for shoplifting in Bristol, then he'd disappear and Fred would never see him again.

"We might need you, to help us in court," he said.

"Yes, but it wouldn't be the same, would it?" Tom argued. "I mean, if I was inside and you had to fetch me all the way up here. Fred would understand that." Of course Fred would. The code of the underworld. When a man's inside, you can't expect him to do anything likely to affect his stay in prison. A man inside can be forgiven many things.

"All right, Tom, I'll see what I can do," Aveyard said. "But no promises. We'll take you down now, put you separate from Fred. When your statement's been typed, we'll have you back to sign it. I'll talk it over with the chief in the meantime, see what we can work out."

"I'd be very grateful, Superintendent."

"Maybe you'd like to be coughing that Bristol job while you're down there?"

"What Bristol job?" Tom asked, his face a mask of innocence. "I'll tell you what, though. Evidence of good faith. I've just remembered the name of the man who meets the landrover each time. It's just come back to me."

"Right. Let's have it."

"Bushden. David Bushden, same as the village."

The map had been marked clearly and showed the village of Bushden. A dotted line with an arrow on it had been drawn up Nether Way South, turning left down Kettering Lane. The line turned left again, into a field track. The outlines of the field had been drawn in pencil, and a figure 3 had been superimposed. There was a ring on the Kettering Lane by the entrance to the field lane, and the dotted line then continued west, away from the village.

"This is where they take the three cows, presumably," the chief said.

"And this is where David Bushden will be waiting to collect his money."

The date on the map was Saturday, the 9th. "That's tomorrow," Aveyard said.

The chief looked at his watch. "You mean tonight," he said.

CHAPTER ELEVEN

Bill Aveyard woke refreshed after his four hours' sleep. He took a long drink from the glass of lemon juice he kept beside his bed. Then he picked up the telephone and dialled the Birton Police Headquarters. When he had identified himself they connected him immediately to the Incidents Room in Bushden Hall. He could imagine the scene in the dining room, the tired smoky feeling that follows a night of duty, constables looking at the clock and waiting for their relief, the table tops littered with paper cups from the coffee machine that always went with them as part of the Incidents Room equipment.

"Roberts."

"Have been on duty all night, Inspector?" Aveyard said, "or are you just coming on?"

"I got my head down for a couple of hours, Superintendent."

"Anything doing?"

Aveyard heard a chuckle at the other end of the line. "What's that phrase, Superintendent, 'we never had it so good?' I'm sitting behind a silver tray, solid silver from the look of it. On it there's a plate of cornflakes, and another of kidneys, bacon and eggs. I could have had kippers if I wanted. The coffee tastes freshly ground to me, Jamaican, I wouldn't be surprised."

"And is that the butler I can hear walking across the carpet. By God, Roberts, there'll be no holding you after this. If you could manage to put down your knife and fork however

and open your Incidents Book I'd be greatly obliged, though
we mustn't let your kidneys get cold, must we."

Roberts was immediately all business. He knew you could
pull Aveyard's leg so far but no further. "It's been quiet.
Very quiet. All the house-to-house questionnaires have been
done but frankly there's not one I want to show you. The
path. report is in but nothing we didn't expect. Nobody's
seen anything of David Bushden. Amanda Tew's been in,
but only to find out if we'd heard anything. Lady Bushden
was in to find out if we were comfortable and of course the
butler was here to take our orders for breakfast. I knew you
wouldn't mind so I let the lads go through to the kitchen for
a nosh up. It seemed to me it would help take Porter's mind
off things. He's been very cut up about that business of
cleaning the carpet but I told him that so far as we were
concerned it was forgotten and forgiven. Oh, there *is* just
one thing. Mr. Victor has identified the plant that was in the
vacuum cleaner as being the same as the specimen he picked
up from the carpet, for what that is worth. He also says the
stain on the back of that letter you sent down is vegetable,
and thinks it came from the plant found on the carpet. He
says he'll let you know definitely about that later this morning. Apart from that there's nothing to tell you."

"Have you heard from Sergeant Bruton yet?"

"Yes, he was on the phone ten minutes ago and he's coming in. I think he fancies the kidneys."

Aveyard put the phone down, and turned over luxuriously
in bed. Saturday morning. He was supposed to be off duty.
Come to think of it he wasn't supposed to be alone in bed.
He'd had quite definite plans for what to do after the pictures last night. But when he arrived home a note was waiting on his sitting-room table. "Dear Bill," it said, "I knew it
was a mistake to get involved with a policeman. I don't
think I can take never knowing what's going to happen, or
where you're going to be. It was great fun while it lasted but

. . . well, I'm sure you understand." She hadn't even bothered to sign the note.

"Damn," he said, and thumped his pillow into a more comfortable shape, snuggling down into the blankets. But suddenly the bed felt hot and lumpy and empty and he quickly got out and went to take his shower. He was thinking of Bushden Hall as he ate his toast. So much wealth, so much privilege, so much possession, and all those cross-currents. A woman still passionately in love with her husband in the evening of their life together, who had not been able to take a trip or a holiday with him for thirty years. Two brothers who hated each other, or so it seemed. One a simpleton, the other an inhuman money-making machine. A house full of servants and gardeners and a butler; a whole village of dependents.

Aveyard had known of Lord Bushden of course. He'd seen him around the county many times, heard him speak from platforms, at openings. He'd read accounts of Lord Bushden's patronage in the newspapers which no doubt this evening would carry full obituaries. But of the man himself Aveyard realized he knew very little. He was prepared to believe that he died of a brain tumour, but why had he asked to see the police? Aveyard knew there was one logical explanation, but somehow he tried not to let it intrude on his mind. If only he could accept that David Bushden had killed his brother Rupert with a vicious slash of the sword, had dropped the sword and then had gone along to tell his father what he had done before fleeing. Obviously his father, a man of honour, would not attempt to conceal the knowledge and would want to reveal it to the police immediately. But would he not also tell his lifelong servant, Arthur Porter? And would he not also tell his loving wife? He was not to know lying there on his death bed whether his second son was actually dead or not. Was that why the bed linen had been turned back? Lord Bushden obviously had had the strength to get out of bed and to put on his dressing gown.

Had he gone along to his second son's room and seen the corpse lying there? Had he been so shocked by the sight that he'd returned to his bedroom and fallen back on his bed to die? Had he ever left the bedroom?

These thoughts thronged Aveyard's mind, bouncing around, crowding out all personal and private thoughts. He knew for example that he had to pick up a suit from the drycleaners, and he needed to do his shopping for the weekend. He knew he had several personal letters to write; he'd promised himself to get the needle on his record player fixed. But he did none of these things. He picked up the telephone again and the Birton Police Headquarters connected him with Dr. Samson.

The doctor's voice was grave. "You've read the report?" he asked.

"No, but I understand there's nothing in it."

"There *is* something in it, Superintendent, and I intend to take this matter up with the chief constable. Mr. Victor disregarded my professional opinion and during last night a full autopsy was carried out on the body of Lord Bushden. You know what that means. The only result of that autopsy was to confirm what I had already said clearly and quite indisputably. Lord Bushden died of a brain tumour exactly in the manner I and the specialists I had consulted had stated he would."

Aveyard was holding the telephone to his ear, listening, but his eyes were gazing at the far wall of his bedroom where he could see, as if in a dream parade, the faces of the men in the cases he'd handled, many of whose deaths would have gone unresolved were it not for the cooperation of the police and forensic laboratories.

He brought his mind back to the present. "It's your privilege to draw whatever you wish to the notice of the chief constable, but for the moment I am the investigating officer of a known crime. I would like to put some questions to you but it would be a waste of your time and mine if those questions were answered in the atmosphere of recrimination you have just created. Are you in a position to give me an unbiased answer to questions about your former patient?"

"That is my duty," Dr. Samson said, "however unpleasant I may find it."

Aveyard felt like telling him to stop being a pompous old bastard and go to hell and for a moment he wondered if perhaps that might not be the best way. But he controlled himself.

"In the few hours immediately before his death how alert would Lord Bushden be?"

"Completely. A brain tumour is a sudden killer. A patient can be right as rain one minute, dead the next."

"Would his physical capacity be impaired?"

"That's harder to say. The tumour could press on part of the brain, and paralyse some of the body. It could take away the use of a person's hand for example or prevent him walking, or even speaking."

"But that had not happened to Lord Bushden?"

"To the best of my knowledge, it had not."

"Thank you for that 'to the best of my knowledge.' It's the most perceptive thing you've said since this case began."

Aveyard put the phone down, not too gently. Let Dr. Samson add that to his list of Aveyard's crimes when he went waffling to the chief constable. At that moment Aveyard was in no mood to care. He put on his anorak and set out for the forensic laboratory in Birton. As his car turned left out of the drive he suddenly thought Dammit, if I'd brought the ticket with me, I could have collected my drycleaning.

The morning was cold but dry, and traffic was already starting to build up with weekend shoppers as Aveyard drove into Birton, turned left at the traffic lights and round the back of the Insurance building that houses the forensic laboratory on its top floors. Few people knew of the existence of the lab; it wasn't the sort of place you advertise. A large lift, against which an ambulance could park to discharge its contents unseen, could be operated only by key and made one stop, where a policeman was in constant attendance. He rose to his feet and saluted when he saw the superintendent.

"'Morning, Ted," Aveyard said. "How's your arthritis?"

"Better, Super, now I'm inside all the time."

"Keep it warm and dry."

John Victor was waiting when Aveyard went into the main laboratory, standing by the two marble-topped slabs, each of which carried a figure beneath drab olive-green dust-sheets. On a side shelf were a number of jars containing organs already pickling in formalin.

"I gave your chap permission to go home for breakfast," John Victor said, "but he didn't seem to have much of an appetite after watching me all night. It's a wonder the way some of your chaps stick it."

Samples of a flower with its leaves had been placed between two glass sheets on the table to the right. John Victor pressed a switch and a diffused light came on beneath them. On the left were a few fragments of dust; the flower was in the centre, and more dust on the right.

"This is the material I picked up from the carpet," John Victor explained. "In the centre is the flower itself. We took that from the vacuum cleaner, dusted it a bit. On the right are the grains from the envelope. I've had them all under the microscope and there are more than sufficient points of correspondence for me to testify they come from the same type of plant. I've also done a quantitative spectrum analysis. All plants differ, you know, in the amounts of inorganic salts they contain. That depends on the soil in which they've grown, the way they've been watered and so forth. These three specimens have exactly the same inorganic salt analysis, and what's more significant, exactly the same nitrogen content. Ordinarily, this would be impossible. Not even two plants grown side by side could have that, because the amount of nitrogen depends on the individual plant's root formation. I'd be prepared to say quite positively they come from the same plant."

"But you can't identify that plant?"

"Not yet. It won't take long, but it's a tedious business of comparison. I just haven't had the time yet. I considered that the name of the plant was less important to you than the fact they were all identical."

"I agree. You've done wonders."

Aveyard looked at the pathologist. He *had* done wonders, working all night, peering into microscopes and test-tubes, at specimens of plants and human beings. What a man to be able to do such a job, to be able to take such a fanatical pride in it. But of course the secret would have to be some kind of fanaticism, like the dedication of a parson with an empty church, who knows he could fill the church overnight by cancelling the services and starting a discothèque for the young folk.

"I'm sorry I couldn't help you more about the two bodies. I've found a whole book of scientific stuff about adiposity in the young man, but that wouldn't help you. The old man was in very good shape considering his age. If that brain tumour hadn't got him, he'd have been good for another twenty years. Shows you the value of eating sparsely and taking plenty of exercise, two things which the young man certainly didn't do."

At that moment the chief superintendent came in. "I guessed I'd find you here," he said to Aveyard. The chief was another advertisement of the value of eating sparsely and taking exercise; he was a big bluff hearty man who spent every available moment in his garden, two acres on the southern outskirts of Birton. His collection of roses was phenomenal.

"We might send Tom down to Bristol," he said, "when this lot is tidied up. We shall need to keep him here to identify the man he and Fred have been doing business with. But

I've had a word with them in Bristol, and they've got a notice on him from Plymouth. He's wanted down there. We
ship him to Bristol where he coughs a shoplifting, they send
him to Plymouth where they throw the book at him."

"There's something I ought to tell you. The chief constable's going to get a complaint from Dr. Samson."

"I've already had it, lad. I think it's time Dr. Samson
thought about retiring. Don't worry yourself about him."

The chief had been walking about the laboratory, examining everything in sight. John Victor gave him the two reports to read and he sat on a stool. A laboratory assistant
came in while the chief was reading them. "Any coffees?"
They all said yes, and he reappeared a few minutes later
with three glass beakers.

"God, what's that been used for?" the chief said, eyeing
his beaker with mistrust. He took a sip of the coffee. "I suppose I'd better not know," he said, continuing to read. When
he'd finished John Victor took the reports from him. "You
write a good one, John," the chief said, "more than I can say
for this idle bugger here."

"I never get the time," Aveyard said.

"Too busy wasting it looking at the Scarlet Pimpernel?"

"I never watch television."

"Not television, you moron. This plant. Under the glass.
The Scarlet Pimpernel. Also known as the Poor Man's
Weather Glass, because the flowers close up at sunset, and
never open in cool weather. 'They seek him here, they seek
him there, those Frenchies seek him everywhere. Is he in
heaven, or is he in hell, that damned elusive Pimpernel . . .'
But I suppose you're too young for Baroness Orczy. Leslie
Howard played the part in the film. He was magnificent,
and if you ask me who Leslie Howard was, I'll brain you."

"They seek him here, they seek him there, those *policemen* seek him everywhere, is he in heaven, is he in hell, that
damned elusive Pimpernel?" Aveyard said, musing. "It

strikes me David Arthur Bushden is pulling our collective leg."

"And he's the man they all thought was a simpleton?" the chief asked.

"He's the man who's going to turn up tonight outside the field gate in Kettering Lane, and collect fifty quid from a man driving a landrover. Guess who the driver is going to be?"

"Jim Bruton could pass for Tom in a dark light. And you, well, you haven't Birmingham Fred's muscles or good looks, but you'll do."

"I get the feeling I shall enjoy myself tonight," Bill Aveyard said.

When Jim Bruton met Bill Aveyard in the Incidents Room, he'd been doing his homework. He produced an Ordnance Survey map of the district, with marks on it. Each mark had a number over it. "These are the reported cases," he said, "but there are bound to be others. I'm having a physical check made of every farm. Have you counted your herd recently? Have you lost any animals? The trouble is that many of them are so bothered by Min of Ag form-filling they may not give completely honest replies. Some of them, you know, aren't always truthful when it comes to declaring the number of lambs or calves born, so they can keep one or two for their own table."

"You've been busy, Jim. Didn't you get any sleep?"

"Enough. My wife doesn't like me, though. I promised to take her shopping in Leicester today."

Aveyard knew Mrs. Bruton well enough to know she wouldn't have uttered one word of complaint. Of all the policemen Aveyard knew, Jim was the one with a wife who'd best adapted herself to the inevitable way of life, the broken promises, and cancelled arrangements.

Bruton pinned his map to the blackboard and easel that were part of their equipment and stood beside the fireplace, incongruous against the dark wood of the panelling and the fine white marble of the fireplace itself. He stepped back and both looked together. The pattern was obvious. The dots formed themselves roughly into a circle, with Bushden at its centre.

"Not very intelligent," Aveyard said. "Why wasn't this map drawn up in Crime Prevention. We pay a sergeant and two constables to think out this kind of thing, to develop trends in crime, to give us forewarning of where a criminal is operating in one particular district."

Organized crime is seldom random. Once a number of break-ins had seemed to follow a pattern of "modus." The same window in the shop, the same method of opening it, the same things stolen. Finally the crime prevention department had drawn the locations on a map. The crimes followed a pattern along one line. At one end of the line a factory worked night shifts. At the other end was a lower-class slum district. They kept watch on the night shift and discovered the men used to play cards during the tea break. One man left work at four o'clock and had to walk home. He lived at "the end of the line." On nights when he lost at cards he broke into a shop on his way home. The police watched and one night, when he'd lost, they followed him, caught him inside the shop where they'd planted men. They'd reasoned this was the next shop in line, the next to be done, and staked it out for three nights running while he had a run of luck at cards.

Somebody, no doubt based in Bushden, or directed by somebody based in Bushden, was responsible for stealing the beasts represented by the dots on Bruton's map.

There was a hole in the map, an area from which no thefts had been reported.

"Let's take a look at those three farms," Aveyard said, "blow some fresh air into our lungs."

The farms were a short way down the Birton road. About a hundred yards after a left turn, the road forked left and right. To the right they could see the gleam of water from the reservoir, surrounded by beautiful evergreen trees of all shapes. On this side of the evergreen belt was the stone farmhouse. Bruton had his records with him. "John Barsly," he said. "Farms two hundred acres for Lord Bushden. A lot of it's potatoes, some arable, and a herd nominally of twenty cows."

Aveyard was looking across the field that sloped up to the evergreen belt. "More than twenty there," he said.

Aveyard drove the car to the farmhouse door. A young boy stood there, eating a sandwich. "If you want my dad," he said, "he's round the back."

Aveyard and Bruton got out of the car, walked round the side of the garden in front of the farmhouse. Behind it were several low long barns built in stone, some covered in old Collyweston slate and all in a good state of repair. Tucked away at the back where it couldn't be seen was a large stone-built beast yard, with a line of beast shelters down two sides. John Barsly was in the beast yard, looking at a heifer tethered to a chain. The heifer appeared to have a bloated stomach. As they watched, John Barsly took a long needle from a wooden case he carried, attached it to a plastic bottle and plunged it into the beast's shoulder. The beast bellowed, but he held it firm between his knees and squeezed the bottle until all the liquid drained into the animal. Then he wiped the pelt with a swab doused in what looked like surgical spirit.

"Shan't keep you a minute," he said, "but you've got to be your own vet these days. Most of them are that damned busy with cats and dogs. Marvellous though, what you can do with antibiotics. A few years ago and this beauty'd be dead."

He finished wiping the beast's shoulder with the swab, then looked into its eyes, opened its mouth and looked in there, then released the beast from its tether and led it into a stall. It immediately sat down on the clean sweet straw. He bolted the bottom half of the door and came back, wiping his hands on the swab he'd used for the beast. Then he packed up his medical box.

"Now, what can I do for you gentlemen. Min of Ag, are you?"

Aveyard smiled. "Not quite."

"Well, one thing is damned sure. You're not the types to be selling cattle food."

Bruton cleared his throat. "We're policemen," he said, "and we'd like to ask you a few questions."

"Fire away, then," John Barsly said, "questions cost nothing."

Bruton looked at Aveyard, who nodded. Bruton would ask the questions, Aveyard would watch the replies.

"Have you counted your herd recently?" Bruton asked.

"Count 'em every day."

"Have you noticed any missing?"

Barsly chuckled. "No, I haven't," he said, "not that I could say the same for some of my neighbours. Jim Skelly, over there on Winstay Farm, lost two he didn't know nothing about until I told him."

"How did you know?"

"'Cos I counted 'em, didn't I. Can't pass a herd without counting 'em. It's second nature when you've been brought up wi' beasts. You know what they say we do?"

"You count the legs," Aveyard said, "and divide by four."

John Barsly chuckled hugely, his big round red face heaving with mirth. He took a handkerchief from the pocket of his breeches and wiped the sweat from his forehead. Aveyard too was sweating; the heat generated by the decomposition of the beast muck in that yard, and the smell, were both overpowering.

"Now, if you don't mind, I'll ask you to excuse me," John Barsly said, "it's time for the groceries, and since I don't have no missis any more, I have to take care of that myself else the bairns would never get nothing to eat, would they?"

As Aveyard got back into the car, he saw Roger Bowman's mobile shop appear. Bowman recognized him, leaned out of the driving seat and waved.

"Look out, you careless bugger," John Barsly shouted at Bowman, "you damn near ran over my toe."

When Aveyard looked back in the driving mirror, the child who'd been waiting at the door had already climbed into the back of Roger Bowman's van.

Saturday in the village, quiet noonday time. Men come in from the cold fields and stand, back to the fire, warming the cords. Time was they'd be in the pubs for pints but the price of that has risen cruel. Time was there'd be a bird in the oven; Saturday was good for peasant poultry, soup to follow for Sunday starters. Time was Birton made Second Division and played worth watching; now it's scrag ends, kickers too puny to transfer, a defence like lace. Women wear curlers in damp hair and look at the schedule of buses they travelled a lifetime, to get him a flanellette shirt on the market, keep his chest warm for the winter. Fingers creased with toil clutch purses and count the new coinage. Watch it, Mam, or a moth'll fly out. The old joke meant love and understanding in the days of poverty, young kids not earning. Now there's money to weight a purse with possibilities, but the new coins don't go far.

Younger men, home from work in a hurry, shout dinner, dash into the yard and tinker with tools. Frank's got a car, bugger him. I'm going to flog this little lot, get myself a mini van, do it up and make a bob. It's a boy's dream; buy cheaply, repair, and sell at a steady mounting profit that one day will send him in for a fuel injection Porsche. What's hope, what's reality? Lend us the use of a hammer, Dad, and I'll put it back. Young girls flounce home from shops and clothing factories. One day I'm going to give that Madam a piece of my mind. Saying my counter was dirty. Donny Osmond mouths something muffled by a plastic box. Turn it down, love, Mam says automatically.

Pheasants in the wood beyond Five Ends make a soothing sound. Old Jim Beddle as was a gamekeeper walks a dog slower than himself, a shotgun under his arm he hasn't fired for five years; pensions don't run to cartridges. He can still see pheasant by instinct, tell you every tree in the wood with a creaking branch needs topping. The earth smells cold and rich as Christmas pudding in January; rooks in the new poplars means the trees are grown to man's estate. Rooks don't settle in a young thing the wind'll whip from under foot. Old Jim smells his surroundings; settles on the grass in any season, under a sack in winter even, wake up eyes closed and tell you where he is. Bushden has no secrets from him. A hedgehog roots by the red campion they used to call hairy arms when old Jim was a lad. Hairy arms. Haven't heard that for a decade or two. He chuckles, and the hedgehog stops. I wasn't laughing at you. What a grand time, the time of hairy arms, working for wages and up every morning at half past five. Who lies in bed when corn marigolds and purple loosestrife scent the morning air, and the earth smells rich?

Saturday morning, noontime, in the village. Jim Beddle stops, reaches into his pocket for a sugar lump. Where are you then, where are you? The old dog looks up at him, pain of walking creasing his eyes. He too searches the noonday field into trees beyond and the wood they've skirted. The field is empty, the field gate closed. "Poor old girl," old Jim says, "don't tell me they've finally taken you." Unbidden tears roll down his cheeks but he doesn't bother to wipe them away. Cold November days take care of that. "Shan't be long for us now," he says. "Us need hardly bother to come back when we follow the Master's box to the church-yard."

CHAPTER TWELVE

"Where next?" Jim Bruton said. Aveyard had asked him to drive the car while he slumped down in the seat, thinking.

"Tell you a name that's kept cropping up," Aveyard said, from somewhere in the pit of his thoughts. "That man Krancek. He knows David Arthur. Maybe he can give us an insight into why a young fellow like that should go bent."

"We don't know he is bent," Bruton said. "We only have Tom's word for it . . ."

"I don't think Tom was lying. Anyway, it'd be too much of a coincidence if he invented a name like that." Bruton was not convinced, wouldn't be convinced until after their jeep ride that night.

Krancek was in his cottage when they arrived in Ice Tower Lane. They identified themselves. He invited them in. The cottage had two rooms, one each side of the centre door. The rooms were low and heavily beamed; the windows were small and leaded and not much light came in. In the room to the left of the main door Krancek had just lighted a fire and the sticks were still crackling. A brass fireguard prevented any burning embers coming out into the room. There was a strong odour of wood smoke and the air was heavy with the scent of burning fig wood. Aveyard noticed a copper basket beside the fireplace in which were split logs and a few dark green branches of fig.

"These old chimneys don't draw too well when they're cold," Krancek said. "They always smoke the place out a bit. If I'm going to smell smoke for half an hour it may as well have a good aroma."

Aveyard was surprised to discover that Krancek spoke such good English. The only way you could have known he was not English born, apart from his appearance, which was typically central European, was in the clipped hardness of his consonants. Midland speech is soft and warm and rich; Krancek took the deep vowels and encased them in hard sounds like steel-jacketed bullets. When he spoke, the words came from his mouth as if from a machinegun. Krancek was wearing corduroy trousers, a dark brown polo-necked sweater and an ex-army windcheater with buttons down the front. His black boots had been carefully cleaned. Aveyard looked at Krancek's hands. Though they were thick and stubby and obviously used to work, the nails were clean and well cared for.

Krancek himself was very clean, close shaven with his hair neatly brushed. The furniture in the room had been bought with an eye for Victorian quality. The dark table in the centre of the room, heavy and solid, had no cover on it but in the middle was an old cruet set, silver-mounted in a silver tray with an ornate handle. Aveyard noticed that the vinegar bottle had been carefully repaired. A piano stood along the side wall with two heavy brass candle sconces which had been fitted for electricity with a brass lamp holder. There was no music on the stand but a metronome stood on the top. The music was in a bow-fronted walnut cabinet behind glass to the left of the piano. The only book whose title Aveyard could read was a collection of the piano sonatas of Beethoven. There must have been a thousand books in the room neatly stacked on dark wood shelves constructed for the purpose. It was the room of a literary, musical, thinking man; Aveyard realized that Krancek himself was a paradox.

"I see you looking round," Krancek said, "and I find surprise on your face! What a man does, need not necessarily represent what a man is. 'They that labour in the fields shall also know grace,' a Polish poet once said."

Aveyard laughed. "I'm sorry if my mouth was hanging open." The fire was drawing now and they sat down at the table.

"You want to know about Mr. David, I suppose," Krancek said by way of an opening. "There's not a lot I can tell you, unless you give me some specific direction into which to point my thoughts. He was a genial young man, and we liked him well."

"We?"

"My wife and I. Did you know I was married? My wife helped to teach the boys at the Hall. Most of these books were bought by my wife. I learned my English from them and from her."

"And David Arthur?"

"He too learned many things from them. I like to think that although many people were brought in to teach him how to be a Lord my wife introduced him to elements of truth and beauty he would not otherwise have known. That may sound pompous but if you're interested in David Arthur you should know he was not just as everyone painted him. He learned many aspects of life from my wife he couldn't have got anywhere else, not even from his father, though Lord Bushden was a truly wonderful man. David Arthur used to come into the greenhouse after my wife died and we talked together. He never played the fool with me. I suppose that was because I never made him any reason to do so. I used to treat him just like any other human being and I think he respected that. He was very interested in so many things . . ."

"I ask myself why you're using the past tense," Aveyard said.

Krancek nodded gravely. "Up at the Hall everyone is using the past tense, even Lady Bushden."

"You've seen her this morning?"

"Yes, she came to the greenhouse. I always supply potted plants for the weekend. She makes the selection herself on a

Saturday morning. She came today to tell me that none would be required. I felt very sad. A few flowers would have cheered her through this long weekend."

Aveyard looked at Bruton who knew instinctively to take over the questioning. He knew Aveyard wanted time to think, to digest the many varied impressions they were receiving of what sort of man David Arthur Bushden was. He looked around the room, searching for some question to ask that would not impede the flow of Aveyard's thoughts. His eyes lighted on the several drawings which hung behind the glass in frames above the piano. "You have very wide-ranging interests," he said, "music and books and architecture?"

"Oh, those are part of what I rather grandly call my Polish Collection," Krancek said, smiling. "I don't think any man can ignore his origin, any more than David Arthur Bushden could."

"Your origins are Polish?"

"Yes, I was a German prisoner of war. My family came from the border area between East Germany and Poland. I've taken an interest in everything I can lay my hands on that comes from there. Take the drawings for example. I found those in a shop in the Charing Cross Road in London. They're part of the design of the castle of Count Opienski, built in the thirteenth century by Czeslaw Czarznormski. He was a very famous castle-builder, though I'm sure you've never heard of him."

Bruton laughed. "I couldn't even pronounce his name," he said. He got up from the table and went to examine one of the drawings.

"Does that sort of thing interest you?" Krancek asked, looking at Aveyard, who sat deep in thought.

"Yes, it does," Bruton said, hoping that would not be the signal for Krancek to ask him technical questions.

Krancek stood beside him and pointed to the drawings. "All these castles," he said, "were very solidly built. Some of these walls were as wide as fifteen feet." He went over the drawing, pointing out the various features it contained—the massive kitchens, the enormous eating room with the spits and the open roasting pit on the edges of which small boys would stand for hours turning a wheel while a whole bullock roasted. Sometimes, when a point of detail seemed to interest Bruton, he would pull a book from a shelf and open at a drawing which showed greater detail. Bruton listened to everything, took everything in, glancing from time to time at Aveyard who was still sitting at the table saying nothing. Finally Bruton judged the time to be right, said "Thank you very much" to Krancek and sat down at the table.

"I've been thinking about your daughter," Aveyard said.

"Matushka? What about her?" Krancek said, immediately wary.

"While I've been listening to you talking to my sergeant I've been impressed by what a careful and thoughtful person you are. You're obviously a man who takes great pride in keeping things proper and correct. I haven't been in your greenhouses, but I don't mind betting they are a model of orderliness."

"That's right," Krancek said, a puzzled look on his face, "but I can't understand what that has to do with Matushka."

"It's just that I can't see a man like you having a daughter who would be slovenly in her work."

An angry flush came to Krancek's face. "You mean this business about the carpet? Porter told me all about that. My girl cleaned that carpet, I'll guarantee that. She's never skipped her work in her life. If there was muck on that carpet then somebody brought it in after Matushka had done her work. I told Porter that. Matushka cleaned that carpet and I don't care who says differently."

"Right," Aveyard said, "let's construct a timetable."

"I can do that," Krancek said, "with no difficulty. Four o'clock: Matushka finished cleaning Mr. Rupert Samuel's room. I know the way that girl works and guarantee that room was hundred per cent neat and tidy. Half past four: Lady Bushden inspects and finds dust on the carpet. Matushka, ordered back to the room by Porter, cleans the carpet again. As you know, when the body of Mr. Rupert Samuel was found, the carpet is once again dirty. Quod erat demonstrandum, somebody was in that room between four and four-thirty and left some dust on the carpet. And then someone was in the room again between four-thirty and when the body was found and left some more dust again."

Jim Bruton had been making notes on his pad while Krancek laid out the timetable.

Aveyard nodded. "Thank you very much," he said. "I think in all probability you are right."

They talked together for a further ten minutes while Krancek gave them information about David Arthur Bushden. His love of the younger man was very clear, as clear in fact as his obvious dislike for Rupert Samuel. He was another who believed Rupert Samuel had held his brother back by harsh cruelties. Finally Aveyard said, "I have only two more questions to ask. Do you believe David Bushden killed his brother?"

Krancek thought for a while and his face creased with sorrow. "I have to tell you," he said, "that I do not think it is beyond the bounds of possibility."

The reply was noted in silence.

"Lastly," Aveyard said, "where do you think David Arthur Bushden is now?"

Krancek thought for a moment. "I do not know," he said, "but I believe one thing, that if David Arthur killed his brother he would not want to stay alive himself."

Now Aveyard knew what had been on his mind throughout this entire interview. "What could this sentence possibly mean?" he asked quickly. "I believe it was written by David Arthur Bushden. 'I go to join those Lords and Ladies we have so often admired together.'"

Krancek knew immediately.

"It means that David Arthur Bushden has killed himself."

"Explain, man, explain," Aveyard said, agitated.

"Lords and Ladies is the name of a wild flower," Krancek said. "It grows in profusion all around the base of the Ice Tower. It was a particular favourite of Lord Bushden. He and David Arthur used to walk and talk together a lot and I have often heard them say, 'Let's go and look at the Lords and Ladies.'"

"But I don't understand you. Why would that mean David Arthur has killed himself?"

"Because the Ice Tower is built over a well. The well has no bottom. It is reputed that an ancestor of Lord Bushden committed suicide by throwing himself into the well. He had just killed his brother."

Bruton was already moving. "I'll get the team," he said.

Aveyard stood up. "And the fire brigade," he said. "I want lots of rope and lights, and get on to the secretary of the Sub Aqua Club in Birton for a couple of divers."

Aveyard and Krancek walked quickly to the Ice Tower which stood in a field behind Krancek's cottage. The tower was round and built of stone, about fifty feet high. A parapet ran all the way around the top. Outside the tower at the back was a windlass which operated a chain of buckets.

"Where are these Lords and Ladies you were talking about?" Aveyard asked, but Krancek shook his head.

"They're not in flower just now," he said. "You'll only find them from late April to early June."

The lock on the door of the Ice Tower had recently been broken open with a heavy stone, which was still standing there. Aveyard pushed open the door carefully with his shoulder. Krancek had brought a torch—with its light Aveyard could see the interior of the room beyond, about twenty feet in diameter, divided into two parts. In the centre of one part a construction made of smooth stones climbed about twelve feet towards the top of the tower. The stones were placed at an angle to each other to form a continuous watershed. On the other side of the room the chain and buckets extended through a hole in the floor about six feet circular around which a small parapet had been built. The buckets went all the way to the top of the tower, and where they turned over the water they contained would trickle slowly down and run over the smooth-rubbed flat stones. Aveyard could imagine that in freezing temperatures ice would quickly form on those stones and could easily be chipped off for use in the Hall: an early form of deep freeze.

He went to the parapet and shone Krancek's torch down into the well. The sides had been bricked for as far as he could see and sloped outwards so that the width below was more than twelve feet. He was careful to touch nothing. There were many footprints in the dust around the well head and the dust on the parapet on the near side had been scuffed.

"This is a considerable antiquity," Krancek said. "The only working Ice Tower still in existence. Lord Bushden had it done up about ten years ago. Must have cost him a fortune. If only he could have known . . ."

Aveyard looked around him, gazing at the cold damp walls in the light which filtered down from above and from the open arches set honeycomb style in the wall starting at about nine feet. He shivered.

"What a place to die," he said.

When the forensic team arrived, the fire brigade, and the volunteer divers from the Birton Sub Aqua Club, they erected ladders going down into the well and shone powerful beams into it. Two divers and one fireman went down. John Victor, who'd been got out of bed, went down with them in a wetsuit the Sub Aqua Club had provided. Aveyard, peering down from the top, could not see what they were doing for the curvature of the well's walls. When John Victor climbed back out of the well he nodded to the fireman who hauled up a bag they had lowered at his request. The bag contained a skull. Aveyard looked at John Victor.

"It's all right," John Victor said. "Whoever this was he's been down there for at least twenty years."

Of the body of David Arthur they had found no sign. "We went as far down as we could," one of the divers said apologetically, "but if he was carrying a weight he is beyond our reach."

CHAPTER THIRTEEN

Saturday evening and the village was quiet. In an age-old superstition no one ventured out alone, but whether they were scared of meeting the malevolent ghost of Rupert Samuel or the benevolent shade of David Arthur it would be difficult to say. Now the local press and stringers from the nationals were in the village in force and the bar of the pub had rapidly filled with them. When they descended on the Ice Tower Aveyard pleaded with them not to trample all over the ground; they had cooperated, and appointed a pool man who was sitting in the Incidents Room now buzzing with telephone calls. What had been a small domestic death now became a matter of national importance and the headlines were already being composed—Where is the missing brother? Is he in heaven or is he in hell? Aveyard cursed when he saw the reference to the Scarlet Pimpernel but was too old a hand to hope any detail of a murder investigation can be kept from the searching eyes of the press. He'd brought them together in the pub. Many knew him to be a cooperative police officer who wouldn't try to hide behind an official "No comment."

"Give me a break, boys," he said. "There's a lot about this one I don't understand—but that doesn't mean I want to see headlines 'Police baffled.' Do me a favour and stay away from the Hall. I'm appointing Police Sergeant Prestwich to be information officer. He'll feed you everything we get. But keep out of sight as much as possible. Don't quote me on this, but David Arthur Bushden may or may not be dead. He may be a simpleton, he may not be, he may be violent, he may not be. But if he sees too much activity going on he may turn into something none of us wants, a paranoic killer. And if any one of you quotes anything of what I've just said, I'll have his guts for garters."

"We've got to have something, Superintendent," one of the journalists said, and Aveyard nodded.

"I know that. I won't see you go away emptyhanded."

Police Sergeant Prestwich walked around the room handing to each man a full plate photograph and two sheets of closely typed information. "Who is he," the caption read, "the missing link of Bushden?" The photographs were very clever reproductions of the skull and Aveyard knew that no picture editor would be able to resist using them.

The local editor of the *Evening Telegraph* smiled at Aveyard. "I've got to hand it to you, Superintendent," he said, "you're the biggest bullshitter in the business. But we'll file the story all the same."

"I thought you might," Aveyard said, smiling.

Aveyard and Bruton left the press conference together. "Might I ask where you're going now, Superintendent?" the man from the *Evening Telegraph* asked, and Aveyard smiled again. "Even a copper needs to go to the bathroom," he said.

They went to Aveyard's flat on the Birton Road and while Aveyard dug in the back of his clothes cupboard Bruton made half a dozen slices of toast and spread on it some of the home-made liver pâté he knew Bill always kept in his fridge. As he wolfed down the first slice he realized neither of them had remembered to eat any lunch.

Aveyard came into the sitting room carrying two polo-necked sweaters the moths had obviously enjoyed and two pairs of thick trousers cut in a style that went out five years ago. Bruton looked askance at the pullover Aveyard offered him.

"I'll be scratching all night if I put that on," he said.

Bill was already eating toast and pâté. "Get it on," he said between mouthfuls. "It'll likely to be a long cold night."

"You think he's going to turn up?" Bruton asked. "All this publicity, all this racketing about in the village."

"I don't know but we can't take a chance. If he's as nutty as we've been led to believe, he could be there. One thing I'm quite certain of—we can't predict anything. Take the case of that note mentioning a wild flower, Lords and Ladies. The forensic boys have checked the ageing of the ink on that note and they can prove it was written not very long ago. But Krancek tells us Lords and Ladies went out of flower six months ago. And anyway, the flower we found, which presumably connects up somehow with this business, is something quite different—a Scarlet Pimpernel."

"So many people have told us what a nice chap David Arthur is," Bruton said thoughtfully, "but yet Krancek, who knew him as well as anybody, says he could have done the murder."

Aveyard put on the sweater and the trousers and his personality seemed to change with the clothing. He even began to look like a young tearaway. "Paradox after paradox," he said. "My mind keeps going round the same circles. It'll be a pleasure to do something for a change."

They drove to Police Headquarters in the park outside Birton. The landrover had been serviced for them and its engine warmed.

"The note said three," Bruton said, as he settled into the passenger seat. "They'd never have brought the landrover for three."

"I know, but this is the only vehicle we've got we can be sure he'll recognize. I don't want to take a chance on turning up in something strange."

They followed the route they knew Fred and Tom would have taken coming from Birmingham. To all casual observers there was no change in the vehicle, but a radio had been installed in the back. It began to squawk. "You've got a couple of earplugs for that?" Aveyard asked anxiously as he drove along the road. "We don't want that noise when we get near." Bruton showed the superintendent two earpieces, the installation of which would automatically cut the loud-speaker.

That night the moon was fitfully bright and Roberts cursed it. He spoke to the men standing round him beneath the trees in the entrance of South Farm, opposite the old vic-arage. "That moon'll make it more difficult, lads, but if I see any of you going up that hedgerow I'll have him on point duty in Birton for the rest of this winner."

They were a motley crew. Some were dressed in khaki trousers and battle-dress jackets, some in shooting gear. One of them, Constable Utley from D Division, had arrived in ski trousers with a black anorak and a hood over his head. He'd even blackened his face with burned cork and the others asked him where he'd left his banjo. They were a branch of the police force the general public knows little about, men who work normally on the routine duty of the police force but have a secondary role when required as an instantly available commando squad. Though it was Saturday night, not one of them would have wanted to be anywhere else. They were fit and highly trained, eager as greyhounds when the rabbit flashes by. Each was carrying a radio netted to the second radio of Inspector Roberts.

"Right, lads, listen in," he said. When he talked into the microphone, each could hear quite clearly, though he only whispered. They'd been briefed that afternoon. Their mis-sion, to form a loose ring through which anybody could pass without seeing them; then, on a signal from the inspector, to close that ring tight and contain any action within. It was a job to which they were accustomed.

Inspector Roberts took his other radio and spoke directly into its built-in microphone. "Able Five to Able One, men starting to move in now."

Aveyard drove slowly along the road, relaxed now he was doing something. Somehow this case had bothered him more than most. There'd been so little to get his teeth into, so little factual evidence for Bruton to assemble for him to interpret, so little substantial information on which they could exercise their minds and professional abilities. He had to admit it; he was floundering for the first time for a couple of years, and didn't like it.

"Do *you* think that was a suicide note, Jim?" he asked, as he drove along.

Jim shrugged his shoulders. "It's a very odd one, if it is," he said. "Especially supposed to be written by a simpleton the doctors all say is beyond help. Such funny wording. "I go to join those other Lords and Ladies . . ." Very stilted, if you see what I mean. I could accept it more readily if it said 'Dear Dad, I don't want the title, I'm off to kill myself.' Or even the classic 'By the time you read this note I shall be dead.' "

"Do you get my feeling it was written as a gag?"

"Well, not quite a gag. I think it's a bit of a try-on, if you see what I mean. Especially since it contained the Scarlet Pimpernel, and not Lords and Ladies."

"If that was the kind of Lords and Ladies he meant."

They had come to the T-junction into Kettering Lane.

"Right," Aveyard said, "now it's eyes down and look in." Bruton reached back and plugged in the two earphones, handing one to the superintendent, who clipped it into his ear just in time to hear the Able Five call signal.

"In position now," Inspector Roberts reported.

"Roger and out," Bruton said back.

Now they were all on listening watch. Now their eyes would be strained to catch any movement in the trees and the hedgerows that shouldn't be there. David Arthur Bushden would be a bloody fool to come tonight, Bill Aveyard thought, but then, some people said David Aveyard thought, but then, some people said David Arthur could be a bloody fool when he wanted.

The figure jumped out of the hedge at them, three quarters of a mile before the trap they had set. He leaped out, waving his arms, blocking the path. Aveyard's window was down and as he braked the landrover the figure came running round the front.

"It's all off for tonight," the voice said, panting and out of breath. "There's police everywhere in the village and it's too risky."

Aveyard swung open his door. He heard the click as Bruton opened his door, too. Aveyard stepped out onto the tarmac.

"Thank God I was able to get hold of you in time," the man said, still panting for breath. "I broke down back there, had to run like hell. We daren't risk taking any animals tonight. I tried to phone you all day, but I could get no reply."

"Good evening," Aveyard said. "My name is Superintendent Aveyard and the man standing behind you is Sergeant Bruton. I wish to put some questions to you about an offence for which you may be charged. You are not obliged to answer any of these questions, but if you do, the questions and answers will be taken down in writing and may be given in evidence."

The man looked at Aveyard, shock registering on his face. He turned round, and saw Sergeant Bruton standing behind him, his arms spread wide. He turned back to Aveyard and suddenly his figure seemed to slump.

"We have reason to believe you may have been assisting other persons to steal cattle," Aveyard said. "I must ask you to accompany me to a police station."

"Get in the car," Bruton said, "and be sharp about it. It's too damned cold, standing out here." He reached into the back of the landrover while the man, stunned, scrambled in.

"Able One to Able Five," he said.

"Able Five?"

"You can all go home. We've caught him. It's Roger Bowman.

"It wasn't my son, was it?" Lady Bushden said. "I knew it could not possibly be David Arthur."

"We daren't take a chance," Aveyard said. The curtains had not been drawn and the night beyond the windows was crusted with the jewels of a million stars.

Lady Bushden had been looking out over the grounds of the Hall. "People laugh at the feelings of a mother," she said. "How many times I've looked out today searching for some indication of my son. But nothing has come to me. I get no feeling that David Arthur is out there, calling for me."

Aveyard was sitting on a chair, a glass of whisky and soda on a tray on the table beside him. He'd hurried of course to tell her that her son was not the man they had captured. She showed no surprise. But at least she had not said, "I told you so."

"I've realized today," she said, "that during David Arthur's life I've always had a feeling of orientation to where he might be. When he was out walking with his father I felt the house was empty of their presence. Whenever I had to go on business or to visit my family, which I did as rarely as possible, I always felt a portion of me was being left behind. Can you understand that?"

"I know what you mean," Aveyard said, "but since I've never been married and had a family of my own, I can't appreciate the depth of it. I take it your intuition is not working now?"

"I think it died," she said simply, "with my husband. I think it was all part of the deep relationship we shared. You know, I've been thinking about that note. When you first spoke of it I was foolish and didn't want to let you know I had not seen it. Most unusual for my husband not to show me something like that. But if it's any help to you, I think I can find a logical explanation for it. I remember once we

had an argument over the dinner table about hereditary
titles, and my husband said how much he admired men who
could forsake the privilege a title gives in order to do a job
of work. I think he was impressed by a man who elected not
to take up his title so that he could stay in the Commons and
not go to the Lords. I was quite surprised by this but my
husband persisted in his admiration of such men though
Rupert Samuel took it very badly, and even I spoke out
against what my husband was saying. I remember poor
Rupert Samuel became quite hysterical. He so far forgot
himself as to call his father a traitor to his class. We had
rather a good wine at supper and I put his extravagance
down to that.

"It was one of David Arthur's good evenings and he took
part in the discussion and said he could understand my husband's point of view. Of course Rupert Samuel turned on him
and said that if he too was turning out to be a traitor he
ought not to have the title anyway. I'm telling you all this
because I think the note could possibly have come as a result
of that discussion, and my husband didn't show it to me because he knew I was opposed to their point of view. I think
David Arthur may have gone to try to make a life for himself
as a common person. Oh, you understand, I don't mean anything disparaging when I say that . . ."

"I know you don't," Aveyard said. "Please go on; you don't
hurt my feelings."

"I think David Arthur has gone somewhere to try to get
himself a job of work to do. He's gone to join "those other
Lords and Ladies we have so often admired together," that
is to say the people who have renounced their titles in
favour of a life of work unconnected with the privileges of
rank."

Aveyard was thoughtful. It was, of course, perfectly logical, and in a sense confirmed something Krancek had said to
him. Krancek was a greenhouse gardener, in a humble job,
lowly paid. But Krancek was also an intellectual and hadn't

he said it doesn't matter what a man does, it's what he is
that counts? And hadn't he said that David Arthur had
learned many things from Krancek's wife? Wasn't that the
sort of philosophy to which an intellectual woman would
cling? It was all perfectly logical. David Arthur Bushden
hadn't killed himself. He'd gone somewhere to make his own
way in life, to get a job, earn his own living and make a man
of himself.

But if that was so, who had killed Rupert Samuel? And
why did Lord Bushden ask to see the police?

CHAPTER FOURTEEN

Sunday morning in the village; the sun rose fitfully and disappeared behind a bank of clouds. The morning was cold. Hoar frost had dusted its white ice everywhere. Old Jim Beddle came out of his cottage on Ice Tower Lane and walked slowly towards the church. A thin plume of smoke rose from Weatherby's cottage and the sound of coughing could be heard from behind Lucas's drawn curtains. Familiar sights and sounds. Jim Beddle's old dog limped beside him, tried to cock its weary leg against the pillarbox, failed to get it far enough and pissed on its foot. "Tha's a silly old bugger," Jim Beddle said, "too old to piss, eh?" The pavement crackled under his foot and the privet bushes that lined the footpath swished as he brushed against them and dropped myriad hoar flakes around his feet. He brought his hands to his mouth and blew into them, seeking the warmth of his breath as he walked along.

Sunday morning old men stir in their beds, grateful for the ending of the night. Mothers wake and cock an ear for baby voices, turn over and revel in an extra half hour of cosiness next to the bodies of their husbands. Men turn over, reach out, and clasp the warm familiar form, hold it, proud with sleep. "It's Sunday morning," young mothers say hopefully and the men grunt. The condensation of night breath pours down the window panes clarifying the frost. The wind moans softly in old tall chimneys and wooden staircases creak. Dogs chase rabbits in their dreams and lay there twitching; cats open their eyes and stare into empty fireplaces, where last night's wood drops potash in a white flurry.

Old Jim Beddle turned into the gateway of the church, walked up the path beneath the slabbed gravestones of the friends of his youth and his family lines reaching back into the ages. He turned left and went round the side to where a small wooden door was set in the thick stone. He opened the door with a key he had taken from his pocket. "Tha'd better stay here," he said to his old dog for the fiftieth time as he started the slow climb up and round the circular staircase. The dog, as was his habit, climbed the first three steps and then lay panting, listening to the slow tread of his master's footsteps as they continued up to the belfry. Jim Beddle stopped outside the belfry door, looking through one of the niches in the wall from which he could see the whole of Bushden laid out below, rising through the dawn mist. Now smoke was coming from the chimney in South Farm, and he saw the milk lorry turn into the Birton Road out of the village. After a few minutes he continued his climb. He opened the door at the top. It creaked and for the twentieth time he resolved to oil it. A pair of eyes gleamed at him from across the bell chamber.

"I know tha's there," he said softly, but he made no move to cross to the dark corner. He turned to the right behind the door and took up a tin of grease and the wooden stick that rested across its top. Two bells hung in the bell chamber. He took the grease and went across to the first one. The lid of the greasing cup was cold but moved easily beneath his hand. He took it off and turned slowly, careful not to look into the dark corner, and using the spatula he smeared grease into the cup to fill it, then screwed the lid back on.

"I know tha's there," he said, "and tha knows tha's got nothing to fear from me." His voice was no more than a whisper but carried into the dark corner of the bell chamber, and when he listened he could hear a quiet rustle. He greased the second bell, then put the tin back on the shelf. He went to the door, pulled it open and turned round.

"Tha's all right here," he said, "tha's quite all right." He went out, shutting the door carefully behind him.

In the dark corner the cat mewed and licked its new-born kittens.

William Tew heard it from Amanda who heard it from Sergeant Bruton in the Incidents Room. William Tew walked round to the vicarage. The Rev. Thomas Dalgleish was in his study putting the finishing touches to the sermon he had written the previous evening for the ten o'clock service. Its text was "Dust to dust, ashes to ashes." It would be a fitting prologue to the eulogy of Lord Bushden he proposed to deliver at the burial service.

"You've lost your organist," William Tew said. "They've arrested him."

"Arrested him? What on earth could he have been doing, the foolish fellow?"

"It was him as was pinching all the cattle we've been losing hereabouts."

"Dear me," the Rev. Dalgleish said, "that hardly seems credible."

"Well, they've nailed him, whether it's credible or not."

The Rev. Thomas Dalgleish put his fingers together. "Who will play the organ?" he asked, but William Tew was already on his way out of the door. He had beer pumps to attend to if he was going to make it in time for church.

Half the village of Bushden turned out for the morning service and Thomas Dalgleish could not believe his eyes when he saw them hurrying up the path. "God moves in His mysterious ways," he said. There had not been so many people in the church since the Remembrance Day ceremony of the previous year when the five neighbouring villages combined forces for the ceremony at the Bushden Cenotaph. He hurried into the church at ten minutes to ten. Fred Latham, the vicar's deacon, was already there, and the numbers of the hymns had already been posted on the board. The vicar went up to the organ loft and switched on the organ motor. The organ blower made its quiet hum and he watched as the pressure indicator slowly rose across the face of the dial. He seated himself at the bench. Just like Roger Bowman to get himself arrested before the service. Why couldn't he have waited until afterwards? the vicar thought petulantly. Now he'd have to play something suitable then rush to the altar to conduct the service. He'd have to change the hymns because it was certain that the people present would not know the tunes. He'd have to think up something they could sing together, if his service was not to be ruined. "Bother Roger Bowman," he said.

He glanced down from the organ loft and now the church was a quarter full. Even old Jim Beddle had turned up and despite the vicar's strictures had brought his dog into the church with him. The dog was lying beside the font. The vicar's heart swelled, remembering how it had been thirty years ago when he was a young curate and the church filled every Sunday morning. This had been his first parish. He'd been here ever since under the living of Lord Bushden. God knew he'd tried. God knew he'd worked hard to make this a Christian parish, not only inside the church but in the village itself, the Youth Club, the Mothers' Union, the Young Wives' Club. It had been a lot of work, but God in His Infinite Wisdom had given His servant Thomas Dalgleish a willing and able ally in the person of His Lordship. For a fleeting second the thought crossed Thomas Dalgleish's mind that God, possibly also in His Infinite Wisdom, had taken Rupert Samuel. Life in the vicarage with Rupert Samuel in the Hall would have been exceeding difficult. But he dashed the thought from his mind as uncharitable, glanced at his watch, spanned his fingers in the chord of B-flat major, and pressed down his hands to begin the worship of the Lord.

The organ exploded in his face at precisely five minutes to ten.

CHAPTER FIFTEEN

"Are there any Irishmen living in the village?" the army major said.

Aveyard looked at Bruton who looked at Amanda Tew who shook her head.

"Did the vicar have any connection with Irish people?" the army major asked.

Again Amanda Tew shook her head. "Not that I know of," she said.

The vicar had been taken to the hospital in Birton and was now in the Intensive Care Unit. His face was badly lacerated by the explosion but as yet they didn't know the extent of the damage he had suffered. The damage to the organ, however, was quite apparent; the whole front had been blown out and forward. Luckily there had been no fire.

The army major pointed inside the wreckage of the keyboard. "This was a very simple type of delayed action bomb," he said, "obviously home-made. When will they stop people being able to buy shotgun cartridges? The bomb was placed in a plastic bag and taped to this plate which forms part of the framework of the organ."

"How was it ignited?" Aveyard asked.

"Very ingeniously, by delayed action. See the ends of this spool of cotton, here? The other end would be mounted in a spring mechanism. When the organ motor was started to work the organ pump, this spool of cotton would rotate with the motor. There must be about a hundred feet of thread here, giving about two minutes of revolution. When all the thread had been wound in, the pin would be pulled, the detonator would fall, the bomb would explode. Very simple, very ingenious. The Irish use them a lot on motorcars."

"It would take a clever man to think that out?"

"On the contrary. This type of mechanism is used for all manner of applications. Many Do-it-Yourself books contain full details of it. It's used, for example, in home-made clock mechanisms, or for flying model aeroplanes—though not, of course, to carry bombs."

"So it could be done by anyone . . . ?"

"Anyone with a practical mind, a pair of skillful hands . . ."

"And an evil mind . . . ?" Bruton asked.

The army major nodded. "That's where you must look, I suppose," he said, "for the person with the evil intention."

"Would it take long to rig?" Aveyard asked, glancing about the church and the organ loft. Anyone tinkering with the organ would be in full sight of the altar.

"Not more than fifteen minutes."

"So anyone with normal access to the church could do it?"

"Ten to fifteen minutes, a roll of sellotape, and something with which to tap that reel on to that spindle . . ."

"What can you tell me about the bomb itself?" Aveyard asked.

The army major and John Victor had spent a half an hour together examining pieces of broken wood, measuring the force of the blast and the direction it had taken. They'd collected many specimens in John Victor's stoppered bottles and the pathologist had taken them back to the laboratory. The fire brigade had been sent away and now only a few members of the congregation, none of whom had been hurt by the explosion in the churchyard outside, whispering and wondering who could have committed such an act of sacrilege in the house of God. Only Aveyard, Bruton and the army major remained inside the church with Fred Latham, the vicar's deacon, standing by the front pew assessing the amount of cleaning and refurbishing that would be necessary, one portion of his mind already busy on an Organ Fund Appeal.

"One thing I don't understand," the major said. "This was a home-made bomb. The explosive used was from shotgun cartridges—I can tell that from this white powder mark on the cast iron frame—but also there was sugar, chlorate and nitrate mixed in with it. The timing mechanism means the bomb was intended to hit a *person*. If all you wanted was to destroy the organ you could fire the bomb with a trip wire or use a simple clock mechanism. But if you were going for a *person* you'd think you'd put something into the bomb, wouldn't you? Something like a handful of nails."

"Thank God he didn't," Aveyard said. "There wouldn't be much left of the vicar."

The major was a large and florid man, about fifty-five, and the chest of his jacket was festooned with campaign ribbons. He hadn't even bothered to put on a battle dress or denims. His hands when he moved them were light and delicate, precise and careful. He exuded an air of efficient confidence. "I've spent most of my service career dealing with bombs of one sort or another," he said. "I was going to study chemical engineering after the last war, but somehow the Services seemed to attract me more than university." He took a large khaki handkerchief from his sleeve, said, "excuse me," turned his head and blew his nose. "With an experience such as I've had, if you'll forgive me saying so," he said, "you go one of two ways or you go stark staring raving mad with these "civil" cases, you either tune your mind on the planting of the bomb and think only of what's happened, so to speak, or you tune your mind on the sort of chap who'd put the thing there. Do you follow me?"

Aveyard looked at him. Behind the façade of the typical army officer he could detect an unusual underlying note. The major wielded the handkerchief again. "One doesn't want to, so to speak, poke one's nose into other people's affairs, but I can't help thinking that if this chap wanted to do damage to *someone*, as distinct from *something*, he'd have gone a different way about it. Yet the affair was rigged to go off when *someone* was there. See what I mean? Doesn't make sense, does it? Fellow who planted the bomb must have been a bit of an idiot, eh?"

Aveyard looked at Bruton. There it was again, the paradox.

"I think he might very well have been," Aveyard said, "though for the life of me I can't see why he would do a thing like this."

Aveyard and Bruton dashed up the front steps of the Police Headquarters in Birton at a quarter to twelve. "Where have they put that chap Bowman?" Aveyard said to the sergeant on the desk.

"I think he's in interview room number three, sir," the sergeant said.

"Who's with him?"

"The chief superintendent, Sir. I believe he is going through Bowman's statement with him."

"Ring through and ask the chief if he'd mind stepping out."

By that time Aveyard and Bruton went up the flight of steps and along the corridor to the interview room the chief was standing outside the door. He didn't speak as Aveyard came up to him. He'd been told about the bomb explosion of course—the assistant chief constable had been visiting in a nearby village at the time and he had gone to the church to see the extent of the damage.

"Can I have a couple of minutes with Bowman?" Aveyard asked. "You'll hardly believe this but I might have a connection with that murder."

The chief put his hand on the knob of the door. "Don't be too long," he said, "I want to prick out my chrysanthemums."

All three went into the room together, a flying wedge.

Bowman was sitting at the table reading the typewritten pages on which, confronted by Fred, he had confessed to being an accessary. He looked up in alarm as the door banged open and the three policemen rushed in.

Aveyard stood in front of the table and, remembering the sight of the vicar being taken on a stretcher into the ambulance with blood running down his lacerated face, he didn't need to pretend anger. "The vicar of Bushden," he said, "has just been injured by a bomb that was planted in the organ. He may live but he may die. You were supposed to be playing that organ. That bomb was meant for you. Right, who hates yours guts enough to want to plant a bomb for you? Who has reason to hate you that much?"

Roger Bowman recoiled in horror. "A bomb," he said, "meant for me?"

"Yes, a bomb in the organ. Now spill it. Who hated you enough to do that, and why?"

Roger Bowman looked wildly at Aveyard, at the chief superintendent, at Bruton, at the constable sitting by the door, but could find no comfort in any of them. He raised his hand to his throat. They had not given him back his tie. He fingered his throat nervously, his mind racing in terror. A look of amazement spread across his features. Aveyard saw it, recognized it for the sudden understanding he knew it to be.

"Who?" he asked, his voice now suddenly gentle. "We want to help you. If he's tried it once he could try again."

"Paul Krancek," Roger Bowman said. His hands came up to his face and tears sprang from his eyes and rolled down his fingers. He was sobbing, but with an immense sorrow for himself. "Who would have thought?"

Aveyard made a small movement with his hands. Bruton brought a chair and slid it silently behind him. Then the chief, the sergeant and the constable went from the room. Aveyard sat down. "Right, let's have it. All of it."

"I stole an anthem out of a book of Krancek's," he said. "I

arranged it and made it into a choral work. That was the one we broadcast. It was only a theme I took, the orchestration was all my own, and after all it's the arrangement and the orchestration that makes a choral work not the tune, not the melody. But when Krancek found out he said some very bitter things to me. He said that to steal a man's creative invention was the worst crime you can perform. That's crazy. Who can tell what's original in music and what isn't?"

"Apparently Krancek could tell. Did he threaten you?"

Now the sobs had subsided. Bowman took his fingers from his face and when he spoke his voice was little more than a whisper, his face incredulous as though he couldn't believe the meaning of the thoughts that flooded him. "Krancek said I didn't deserve to live," he said, and then the tears started again. "He said the organ should blow up right in my . . . face . . ." He exploded in a flood of tears and his face went down and Aveyard quickly pulled the typed statement from the top of the table; the tears were falling onto it. Aveyard got up.

"I can't understand men like you," he said. "You're bent. You have the makings of a good little business with customers who trust you and give you the means to earn a good living and yet you bend that trust by stealing their cattle. You have a God-given gift of musical ability and yet you bend that gift by stealing other people's creative efforts. You've got a good healthy body and a good healthy mind and yet you bend it by pouffing around the place. God, how I hate men like you." Aveyard turned around, walked to the door and opened it. "He's all yours, Chief," he said.

The chief put his hand on Aveyard's arm. "I know exactly how you feel, lad, but this is neither the time nor the place. Go and find young Bushden."

Aveyard was silent as he walked along the corridor of the Police Headquarters. There were so many ways in which the police could be useful in a community, so many important things he would like to be doing, but here he was on a Sunday morning wasting his time on a man who would never know right from wrong. Men like Roger Bowman could only give Aveyard an intense anger which he knew somehow he must learn to control.

"Let's go and see Paul Krancek again," he said to Bruton. "Only this time let's get the full story."

Matushka Krancek opened the door.

"Is your father in?" Bruton asked.

A voice called from within. "Is that the policeman again? Come in, come in." Krancek was sitting at the table in the room in which they had interviewed him before. "Take a seat. What can I do for you?"

Matushka was hovering in the doorway. "You ought to offer them something, Dad," she said.

"Offer them something?"

"Yes, tea or coffee or a drink."

"You think I've lived all this time in England and don't know the English ways, my girl," Krancek said, his face smiling. "These are two policemen on duty and policemen on duty in England don't take refreshments with people they intend to interrogate. You get on with the dinner. I want to eat at one o'clock." He turned to Aveyard. "You do intend to interrogate me, don't you? You have that angry look in your eyes." Krancek was no fool and intended the policeman should know it.

"If you know so much about the habits of policemen," Aveyard said slowly and deliberately, "you'll recognize the words I am going to speak. "As soon as a police officer has evidence which would afford reasonable grounds for suspecting that person has committed an offence, he shall caution that person or cause him to be cautioned before putting to him any questions relating to that offence.'"

"You recognize the flaw in that statement?" Krancek said.

"Yes, I do, full well," Aveyard replied. "What are reasonable grounds for suspecting? Let us take a hypothesis. Let us suppose a bomb has exploded in a church—I'm only supposing, mind you—and the person for whom that bomb was intended has been threatened. Let us further suppose the threat said, 'I wish that organ would blow up in your face' . . ."

"Ah, but that's not a threat," Krancek said. "That is more a statement of desire. If the man had said 'I will cause that organ to blow up in your face,' you would have your reasonable grounds for suspicion. As it is, I don't think you've got anything at all. I'm quite sure any lawyer I might engage in my defence, assuming I needed a defence, would feel obliged to draw that fact to the attention of the judiciary."

"Touché," Aveyard said. Now his humour was restored. This was the sort of game he enjoyed. "Right, let's drop the official caution approach and let me ask you some straight questions in the hope of getting some straight answers. Have you ever played the church organ?"

"Never," Krancek said.

"If we find your fingerprints on the organ, we shall have reasonable grounds, shall we not?"

"You will."

"Have you been inside the church since the time the organ was last played? . . ."

Krancek was shaking his head from side to side. "How could I know when the organ was being played?"

Aveyard chuckled inside himself but no sign of that appeared on his face. Now Krancek felt superior and confident and that, Aveyard knew from experience, could be his undoing.

"Do you take sugar in your tea?" Aveyard asked. Krancek said no, surprised.

"Does Matushka take sugar in her tea?" Krancek said no again.

"Do you keep sugar in your house?"

"Of course," Krancek said, "we keep some for cooking, I imagine."

"Are your purchases recorded at the shop?" Aveyard asked. "Do you have one of those books and order your groceries weekly?"

Krancek nodded.

"Did you ever buy anything from Roger Bowman's shop?"

Krancek shook his head vehemently. "I wouldn't have anything to do with that man," he said.

"Because he stole some of your music?"

There it was. Krancek realized he'd fallen right into it with all this business about the sugar and the book. Bruton was smiling in admiration. He'd heard Aveyard do it a score of times. Now he knew Krancek would be discomfited.

"If you think I would be crazy enough to make a bomb and plant it . . ."

"Hang on," Aveyard said. "Did I say anything about making a bomb?" Did I say anything about a home-made bomb?"

"I just naturally thought since the bomb was planted in the organ at the church . . ."

"Hang on," Aveyard said, "I didn't say anything about a bomb being planted in the church."

"But you said earlier . . . about the organ blowing up."

"It's not what I say that counts," Aveyard said, "it's what you don't say. We can find out if your fingerprints are on that organ or what's left of it. We can find out if you've been buying sugar, if you have access to sodium chlorate. I can take your photograph to every chemist's shop for fifty miles around to find out if you've bought shotgun cartridges."

Aveyard's voice bored on, grinding steadily at Krancek. Aveyard knew there was something Krancek was not saying. He also knew that Krancek hadn't planted the bomb. He wasn't that sort of man. Certainly, East European, away from his homeland, he was the prototype of the bomb-chucking anarchist, but anarchists don't surround themselves with Browning and Shelley and Keats and Johnson, anarchists don't spend their time doing tracings of old Polish armorial bearings. Krancek had not planted that bomb but he knew something, that was certain, and Aveyard was determined to find out what it was.

He got up and turned to Bruton. "Come on," he said, "let's leave this smart alec alone. Let's come back when we've found the fingerprints and got a few identifications. When we've done that we can start chucking our weight about."

Bruton admired the superb performance. Bill Aveyard ought to be with the Northampton Rep.

Bruton stayed where he was. "Hang on a minute, Superintendent," he said, "let's give Mr. Krancek a chance."

"A chance?" Aveyard said brusquely. "To do what? To play word games with us? I don't need this kind of messing about."

"Wait," Krancek said, "it's not for myself, you understand. I loved that boy like a son. Have mercy on him. Don't unleash your bloodhounds. Oh, I know you can find it all, the fingerprints are bound to be there, he won't have been clever enough to cover up his tracks when he bought the sugar and the nitrate. He got the sodium chlorate from me. I keep a large tin of it in one of the greenhouses. He got it from me before when he made the fireworks. It was only a joke. The fireworks I mean. The organ in the church—I didn't know anything about that. Believe me I didn't know! I would have stopped it. Each of us is dependent on every other one. He was the only person I could talk to. Sometimes I think I talked too much to him. I treated him as a normal rational human being, but the poor fellow, no matter what you may have seen from time to time, wasn't normal. He wasn't rational."

Aveyard had sat down again and now was listening intently. It had been a cruel thing to break this man down by histrionics but it had to be done. "You mean David Arthur?"

"Yes."

"You told him about Roger Bowman stealing the anthem?"

"I never thought . . ."

"You said to him, 'I wish the organ would blow up in his face?' "

"Honestly, I never thought . . ."

". . . he would translate your words into deeds? The simple-minded can't dissimilate," Aveyard said. "Word and deed follow each other with a terrible logic in the simple-minded."

"I know that now."

"You still don't know where David Arthur may be? You still believe he's in the well below the Ice Tower?"

Paul Krancek nodded. "Yes," he said, "that's where I think he is. May God be merciful on his immortal soul."

CHAPTER SIXTEEN

Impressions crowded Aveyard's mind as he and Jim Bruton walked across the field from Krancek's cottage. It was one o'clock, lunchtime, but neither felt like eating.

"It's all there somewhere, Jim," Aveyard said, "if only we could find the key to it. David Arthur and Krancek are friendly. Krancek innocently says he wishes the organ could explode in Bowman's face and David Arthur is simple-minded enough to do something about it. We know he could make a bomb from what we learned in the pub about the fireworks—he'd have no difficulty getting shotgun cartridges for it . . ."

"On thing that has been bothering me," Bruton said, "and I curse myself for not making the connection sooner. You remember that in the list of things Fred Latham said David Arthur had bought was a pound of sugar. I never thought anything of it at the time but I ought to have. After all, what would he want with a pound of sugar? They must buy groceries in bulk for a place as big as the Hall and I can't see Porter saying to the young master 'nip out and fetch us a pound of sugar.'"

"You're right, of course. Both of us ought to have seen that one and asked ourselves why. We'll now take the case of the murder of Rupert Samuel. Again, it's a case of simple-minded cause and effect. David Arthur admired his father. His father approves of those other Lords and Ladies who gave up the title. Rupert Samuel didn't approve, called his father and David Arthur traitors. No doubt after Matushka had cleaned that room, David Arthur went up there and he and his brother had a bit of a row. Even maybe a bit of a scuffle. David Arthur loved plants and had maybe taken up that Scarlet Pimpernel, and they had a bit of a scuffle and the Scarlet Pimpernel was dashed onto the carpet. Well, enough of it to make the carpet look dirty. Then the two brothers went out somewhere together and Lady Bushden came in and saw the dirt on the carpet and the cleaning girl was brought back. Then the two brothers came back. David was probably still carrying that Scarlet Pimpernel. But now of course he's flipped his lid and he has the sword in his hand . . ." He looked at Bruton who was shaking his head.

"That doesn't hold much water," Bruton said. "Rupert Samuel was no fool. If David Arthur had picked up the sword from the top landing, he'd guess what he wanted it for."

"You're quite right," Aveyard said. "Well, perhaps Rupert Samuel went back on his own and David Arthur went somewhere and brooded about it and then he thought, to hell with him, walked along the top corridor, picked up a sword, went into Rupert Samuel's room and hit him with it."

Again Bruton was shaking his head, carrying out the function he knew Aveyard required of him. "That doesn't make sense either," Bruton said. "That's a two-handed sword. He couldn't have carried the flower in with him and we know the flower wasn't already there because the carpet had been double cleaned." They had reached the Ice Tower.

"A flower and a sword," Aveyard said, "and somehow we can't put the two together."

A policeman was standing outside the door of the Ice Tower. He sprang to attention then pushed the door open for them. They went inside. The forensic team had finished in there and all the apparatus had been removed. "If he's in there," John Victor said, "he's gone down with a weight around him and we'll never get him back." Aveyard and Bruton walked to the edge of the well, looking down into the darkness. Aveyard did not know why they had come, but somehow he felt a strong affinity with this cold deserted place. He looked around at the archways that had been cut in the thick walls, looked up at the parapet at the top of the walls. The Ice Tower was not roofed over and daylight filtered down from the top. He shuddered, thought again of the skull they had found. What a place to die. Stones of one wall formed a pattern where at one time there had been a doorway. He looked round and saw several such walled-in doorways.

"I suppose people used to hide in here, once upon a time," he said. The place was dank with bygone fear for him. He could almost see the men who'd used this place as a lookout, as an observation tower, as somewhere to cower against the fears that would surround them in Reformation England. Hadn't Amanda Tew said this part of the world was very active in the days when to worship God in the Catholic faith was sinful? Aveyard was no historian. He couldn't tell you the date of the Reformation, couldn't tell you under which of the many rulers of England the terrors had taken place. But he could still experience the horror of confinement the men must have felt.

"You could hide a whole regiment in these walls," Bruton said, "like in the walls of those old Polish castles Krancek was showing me. God knows how many secret rooms there would be, all connected together like a rabbit warren, with doors on the inside and the outside so that people could get in or out without the fear of being caught." He fell silent for a moment and Aveyard thought that Bruton too had been affected by this place.

"I suppose we could get somebody with deep diving gear and send them to look for the bottom of that well," he said, "but somehow I don't want to do it, not yet." Bruton didn't reply. Aveyard glanced at him, and saw that he was lost in thought.

He put his hand on the sleeve of Bruton's jacket. "Come

on," he said, "let's get out of here before it gives us both the willies."

They walked together down Ice Tower Lane and turned to go up to Bushden Hall, neither of them speaking. When they came to the junction of the High Street and Hall Way Bruton stopped. "Do you need me for a quarter of an hour, Superintendent?" he said.

Aveyard looked at him, surprised. "Not particularly," he said.

Bruton gave an embarrassed laugh. "It's just a thought I've had," he said.

Aveyard understood. Jim Bruton wasn't the man to go off without a reason. "Righto," he said, "I'll see you later." He paused for a moment but it was obvious that Jim wasn't going to move until Aveyard did. Aveyard shrugged his shoulders and walked up Hall Way. Bruton watched him go before he turned back down the High Street.

When Aveyard got back into the Hall just after one the forensic report waiting for him contained nothing new. The bomb had been home-made from materials that could be procured anywhere. There were no fingerprints, nothing to give a clue as to who might have planted it. A report from the hospital said the vicar was out of danger and had been removed from the Intensive Care Unit. The damage to his face would heal and he would not lose the sight of his eyes. His face would show the pockmarked effect of the blast but it would be no worse than if he'd had an attack of smallpox. There were so signs of David Arthur Bushden.

The second forensic report was more interesting. It contained a further confirmation that Lord Bushden had died of the brain tumour in the chemical analysis of the cerebral fluid and a statement that Rupert Samuel had died of a single blow from the sword. A number of calculations showed that the sword weight was consistent with the depth of the cut and that the blow could have been struck by anyone with sufficient strength to raise the sword above his head and swing it. The calculations also showed that the wound was not inconsistent with a one-handed blow. One fact that had emerged solved one of the problems in Aveyard's mind. John Victor had measured the depth of cut at the front and the back and could make the following predictions: if the assailant were taller than the victim the blow must have been struck from the rear since the indentation of the cut was deeper at the front than at the back. For the assailant to have struck the blow from the front he would need to have been shorter than Rupert Samuel's 5 feet 10 inches. Aveyard quickly added a speculation of his own to that. It was exceedingly unlikely that Rupert Samuel would have stood still and permitted someone to hit him with the sword, therefore it seemed most likely that the blow was struck from behind, and therefore, quod erat demonstrandum, the assailant was taller than the victim.

"I want you to find out the height of everybody connected with this case," he said to Inspector Roberts. "Anybody who's under five feet ten you can forget."

Inspector Roberts made a note in the book.

Aveyard asked to be connected with John Victor. When he heard the familiar voice he said, "Two questions. Firstly, how can you be sure that the blow on Rupert Samuel's neck wasn't struck by a shorter person standing in front of Rupert Samuel with his wrist bent upwards?"

"Think about that," John Victor said, "think about where the sword would go after the blow. Obviously it would be dragged down the front and the front of the wound would show a slice. But that wound was clean and straight and it didn't show any slice either at the front or at the back. What's your second question?"

"The position of the body on the carpet when you found it. Is it possible that when the body fell it twisted through 180 degrees? The body was facing the door."

"That's perfectly possible," John Victor said. "Most bodies

twist when they fall. It's easier for a body to twist than to break at the knees. It's quite possible that whoever came in carrying the sword found Rupert Samuel turned away from the door; they could have hit him before he was aware that they were in the room."

"But surely he'd have heard them come in?"

"Not necessarily. I suggest you go back upstairs and check that door. You'll find it opens silently, and since the floor is carpeted one could easily get in and across it without a noise. I know, because I tried it."

Aveyard cursed himself; he ought to have tried it too. He put the phone down. One thing he could try and did. "Stand up," he said to Inspector Roberts, "and turn your back to me. When I tap you on the shoulder I want you to fall down as naturally as you can."

"What's this?" Inspector Roberts asked. "Karate lessons?"

"You'll see," Aveyard said. Inspector Roberts turned his back. "Watch it when you tap me," he said, "I'm not getting danger money you know." At that moment Aveyard's hand landed on his shoulder and Inspector Roberts promptly fell to the ground. When he landed he was facing the superintendent and Aveyard saw that the inspector's knees had twisted naturally as he went down.

The inspector looked up at him from the parquet floor of the dining room. "Can I get up now?" he said. "Or are you going to fetch a sword and try that out too, because if so I think I'll stay where I am."

Aveyard held out his hand. "No, you can get up now," he said. "I've made the point I wanted."

The inspector grinned as he climbed to his feet. "When I read that report I tried it out on Constable Bigby and his knees twisted too."

"Why didn't you tell me?" the superintendent said. "You could have saved yourself a bit of bother."

"I know you like finding things out for yourself," he said. He sat down behind the Incidents Book and Aveyard was reminded of the Bible on the vicar's lectern. "I won't enter the experiment in the book," the inspector said. "They might charge you with assaulting a junior officer."

Aveyard sat in his chair looking at the papers on his part of the long dining-room table. So much paperwork with any crime, and this was no exception. So many facts to be gathered, and who could tell in advance which would prove to be the important ones. He began his usual practice of making a mental catalogue of the things that had been done and the things that remained yet to do but the thought uppermost in his mind was find David Arthur Bushden or verify that he is in fact dead.

The door opened and Amanda Tew came in. She walked across the dining room to where he was sitting, a look of interrogation on her face. There was nothing he could tell her. She wouldn't be interested in the chemical analysis of cerebral fluid.

"I've been thinking. I don't know if it will interest you, but I have the feeling it's been a bit tense around here for the last few days ever since we knew that Lord Bushden was dying."

"You would expect it to be tense," he said. "Are you trying to suggest it was something different from the normal expectation of death?"

"Yes, I am. I have the feeling there were deep undercurrents. Mostly I'd say coming from Rupert Samuel. David Arthur was bothered, of course, by the thought that his father was dying. They were such good friends, you see, but it was nothing more than what you might call a normal sadness. Somehow, now I come to think of it, Rupert Samuel was different. For a start he wasn't so bad towards his brother. He almost seemed to be trying to make a friend of him, as if he was making up for all the bad years now that their father was dying and they would both be alone together, left alone together if you see what I mean. Once or twice I came across them and they were talking together very confidentially. They would be quiet when I came, and very unusually, David Arthur wouldn't tell me what it was all about. That's very strange because David Arthur always confided in me, especially when Rupert Samuel had been talking to him. He didn't seem quite so friendly towards me. I began to wonder if perhaps Rupert Samuel might be trying to turn him against me." She gave a nervous laugh. "Oh," she said, "you probably think I'm just imagining it."

She got up and went out of the dining room, embarrassed, or so Aveyard thought, at having betrayed some of her secret thoughts. Inspector Roberts watched her go, then came to Aveyard's chair. "Porter was asking about lunch," he said.

"We don't want to be a bother to him."

"Normally I would agree, but he still feels bad about that vacuum cleaner, you know, so I took the liberty of telling him he could do something if he wanted."

"What you're trying to say is, can you have your dinner now, eh?"

"Well, I'm sure there'll be plenty . . ."

"What is it, caviar . . . ?"

The inspector looked embarrassed. "Actually, it's pheasant pie. Apparently, the cook makes a bit of a speciality of it. Of course, he got her Ladyship's permission to serve wine with it, but I drew the line at that."

"I'll bet a few of the bottles in this cellar would be well worth tasting."

"If you fancy a drop of something, I'm sure the butler would be only too pleased to pull a cork or two . . ."

Superintendent Aveyard got out of his chair. "Stop it, Inspector," he said, "this is a murder investigation, not a punting party on the river. Have your pheasant pie, but the first lad I see with a wine glass in his hand . . . on duty . . ." He was just going out of the room when Sergeant Bruton came in. There was an eager look on his face. "Don't tell me you've come for the pheasant pie," Aveyard said.

"Pheasant pie, that's a good idea . . ." Bruton looked at Inspector Roberts who was shaking his head desperately behind the superintendent's back. "If you care for that sort of thing," Bruton added, hastily.

Aveyard snorted and went out into the hallway. Bruton followed him.

"I was thinking," he said, "and I went to check up on something."

Aveyard turned to him. Bruton was a man for facts, not for unnecessary speculation. "Thinking what about?" he said.

"You know the Priests' Hole where the two lads used to play?"

"Behind the panelling?"

"That's it. When they built these Priests' Holes, they gave them a way in, *inside* the house or castle, and a way out, *outside*."

"We didn't find a way out . . ."

"That's right. So I went to see Krancek again, studied some of those drawings he has. Often they built those Priests' Holes with a couple or three rooms, all connected. But *always* they gave them a way out, so that if anybody started battering down the panelling, the priests wouldn't be caught like rats in a trap. Where's the way out in this one?"

Already Aveyard was walking along the corridor. He reached the panelling, pressed the piece of dowelling the butler had showed him and held in the other key. The door slid open. They went through the panelling into the Priests' Hole, turned on the light, stood there, looking round, examining the walls and the ceiling. The walls were made of stone, solidly mortised together. Aveyard drew his finger down each of the faint cracks which showed. There were no traces of any deeper slit, anything that might indicate an opening. Across the far corner of the room was the construction on which a bed would be laid. He took off the dunlopillo mattress with its cover. The bench revealed was solid and flat. Baffled, he stood erect in the centre of the room and looked about him again. Sergeant Bruton was looking at the floor.

"Let's have this carpet up," he said. When they had put the table on the bed construction they rolled the carpet from the edge of the room. The exit was in the centre of the floor beneath the carpet. They wouldn't have spotted it immediately but a sprig of what Aveyard now knew to be Scarlet Pimpernel had caught between the stone and the surround.

"Get the butler," Aveyard said.

Bruton hurried out of the Priests' Hole.

Aveyard examined the square of stone. Somewhere in the room, he guessed, would be a means of opening the floor. But where? Obviously it would be well hidden so that it could not easily be found by the people persecuting whoever was hiding in here. But where could it be? He pressed with all his weight on each corner of the stone but, as he expected, it did not move. He searched the walls again, rapidly. Then he looked carefully at the hinges of the door, the only metal fittings the room contained.

One hinge was false. The lower one of three. It looked just like the other two hinges, obviously blacksmith-forged, but it wasn't connected to the door. By putting his fingers between it and the door, Aveyard was able to prise the hinge away. The joint of the hinge was effective only at the bottom; when he opened the hinge and pulled downwards, a length of rod was revealed, emerging from the bottom part of the hinge like the handle of a bicycle pump. The hinge strap went down about forty-five degrees before it stopped. Aveyard looked back at the slab of stone. It had not moved. Disappointed, he crouched over the stone and pressed each corner again. Perhaps the hinge operated a bolt, a metal rod that held the stone in position. But still he couldn't move the stone.

Bruton and the butler came in. The butler was wearing an apron in navy blue with white stripes.

"I was helping the cook," he said, seeing Aveyard look at his apron.

"Never mind about that. Did you know there was a way out of this room?"

The butler was astounded. "A way out? I never knew that."

"We think there's a way out. Here, in the floor. You don't know how to open it?"

"I'm afraid I don't. I didn't even know it was there. Dear me, a way out. After all these years. No wonder I couldn't find them sometimes. The young rascals!"

"There must be plans of this house," Aveyard said. "Architects' drawings, that sort of thing. Any idea where Lord Bushden kept them?"

"In his office."

"Which is where?"

"The room on the right just inside the front door."

They went to the office and Porter showed them a large cupboard. Inside it were a number of drawers, each labelled. One, fortunately, said PLANS. Aveyard pulled out the drawer which was three feet wide by a couple of feet, and about twelve inches deep. The plans were all there. House plans, plans of the grounds, the estate, plans of each dwelling on the estate. Aveyard took out the manila folder labelled House Plans. He spread it out on the desk and opened it, searching rapidly for anything that might indicate the Priests' Hole. Eventually he found a plan of the ground floor, folded four times. When he opened it out it showed each room. The plan itself had been drawn by an architect and the script on it indicated a considerable antiquity in the flowery curlicues of the lettering. However, someone had printed the Priests' Hole on it, superimposed on a space that indicated an outer wall. A fine line extended to the margin. It touched a box in which had been printed, in modern script, "Site of Priests' Hole, approached from door concealed in back hall." It also gave the secret of opening the door, with a small drawing of the section of dwelling to be pressed.

They went outside the house to the back wall, standing at a point beneath where they guessed the Priests' Hole to be. The house had been set on a slope and the ground floor at the front was the first floor here. There was a small circular back drive, a door leading to the kitchen area and the tradesmen's entrance. Out at the back were several separate outhouses, and Porter explained each one. "That used to be the bakery," he said, "and that was the laundry. That was the pump room when the water came from the well. Imagine, a young lad spent his entire working life in that room, just working the handle of that pump backwards and forwards. You couldn't get anyone to do that now, no matter how much you paid them."

"I thought it was always carried about the house in pitchers?" Aveyard asked. "Along with the buckets of coal."

"It was, before the house was piped. This was one of the first houses to be piped and have pumped water."

But Aveyard was not interested in pipes or pumps or water. He was examining the wall of the house. To his right, a small barred window.

"Where does that lead?" he asked.

"Into the back larder. We use it for game."

Aveyard looked up to the heavy stained window he had seen at the back of the hall, near the door of the Priests' Hole. "And that's the back of the hall?" Porter nodded.

Bruton looked up, measured the wall with his arm. "I would say the Priests' Hole came out here," he said. They examined the wall together but could find no trace of a hidden door. "Of course, there could be a long passageway under ground," Bruton said. "The exit could be anywhere. On Krancek's drawings, some of them had corridors half a mile long. Some even went under the moats of castles and came out in copses specially planted nearby." He looked around and both saw the large number of trees not a stone's throw from where they were standing.

"Ask Inspector Roberts to get a team of men busy looking for a way out," Aveyard said. "It could be anything; in the ground, in the trunk of a tree, anything unusual."

"Inspector Roberts," Porter said, his hand going to his mouth. "I've forgotten to take him his pheasant pie. Cook was dishing it up when your sergeant called me."

"He'll have to go hungry for a while," Aveyard said, all copper. Bruton had already set off round the house. Aveyard followed him, went back to the Priests' Hole. He stood there, looking down at the stone slab in the floor, thinking. It should be possible to work it out, shouldn't it? There was no ring set in the top of the stone, so no way of lifting the stone. He worked the handle of the hinge again, and the pin slid into and out of the barrel of the hinge with ease. It had no doubt been oiled by the boys, and there was no damp in the room. Obviously the slab wouldn't swivel with weight alone on it because somebody might put his foot on it. Somewhere there had to be a mechanism to cause the slab to list, or something to make it slide. But if it slid, where would it slide to? The stones on each side were firmly fixed; Aveyard had tested them.

He was still looking down at it when Bruton came into the room. "Inspector Roberts has sent half a dozen lads out looking," he said. "They'd just come back from the house-to-house questioning about the bomb."

"How would you do it, Jim?" Aveyard asked. He showed the sergeant the hinge. "I thought this might be the way to lift the stone, sort of a hydraulic jack, but it doesn't seem to have any effect. I think there's probably a pin going into the side of the stone to lock it, but that doesn't tell us how the stone is lifted."

"Perhaps the stone slides?" Bruton suggested.

"I thought of that, but where does it slide to?"

Bruton contemplated the stone and then he placed his

foot against it and pushed. The stone didn't move. "Do you reckon it's a crowbar job?" Bruton said.

"No, I don't think so. These things were all skillfully made. Remember, Porter suggests the two lads knew how to open it and they can't have had much strength to use a crowbar. It must be something more simple than that." He looked at the hinge, at the stone slab. "Hang on a minute," he said, "I've got a bit of an idea." He went to the door and closed the hinge. Then he opened it again, but only half-way. He went back to the stone and tried it. The stone didn't move. He was on his knees looking down at the crack when Bruton crawled across to where he was.

"Hang on," Bruton said, scrambling away from the slab he was kneeling on, next to the one they had assumed was the hidden door. "I felt this one move, just the merest fraction of an inch." Together they pressed the other slab.

"It *is* moving slightly," Aveyard said. "It seems to want to tilt."

He got up and went back to the hinge. "Now," he said, "while I move the hinge slowly, you press down on the slab." He closed the hinge all the way and Bruton exerted all his force downwards. Then Aveyard slowly opened the hinge. When he reached an angle of about thirty degrees, suddenly the slab Bruton was leaning on tilted about half an inch, the edge level with the suspected door rising while the opposite edge fell.

"I think I've got it," Aveyard said. Keeping the hinge in its thirty-degree position, he pushed it downwards. Now he could feel a resistance to his downwards stroke. He exerted a little more pressure, and suddenly Bruton shouted, "It's going, it's going."

Aveyard looked back. The slab was starting to move, and the slab next to it was tilting, like a folding shutter that bends back upon itself in accordion pleats. The full downwards movement of the hinge pushed the slab all the way over, revealing a hole beneath and an iron runged ladder set into the wall. "You have to get that hinge just right, so that it connects with the hydraulic mechanism," Aveyard explained.

"They knew about hydraulics in those days?" Bruton asked, amazed.

"Have you never seen the drawings of Leonardo da Vinci?" Aveyard asked. "He had a complete working model of a hydraulic system . . . and he was fifteenth century. Or thereabouts . . ."

When Bruton came back from the Incidents Room he'd optimistically brought a torch with him. He handed it to the superintendent, who climbed down the iron runged ladder. At the bottom was a room about ten feet square. He shone the torch up the ladder so that Bruton could see to descend. The air down there was stale, and moist. No breath of wind to suggest a window or an opening of any kind. Aveyard shone the torch around and saw a door leading off the small room. It was fastened by three iron bolts. He opened them one by one, then pulled the heavy close-fitting door open. The light of a candle came out at them as they opened the door.

A young man was sitting in the room beyond the door, eating from a tin of beans at a table, sitting in a heavy wooden chair with a canvas back. There was a bunk across one wall, and a table across another. Candles had been set in niches on the wall; three were alight. Aveyard noticed the packets of candles stacked on the table top, the box of provisions, tins and packets. The used tins had been stacked neatly against the wall on the floor. A curtain hung across one corner; Aveyard guessed that behind it would be a chemical closet, and no doubt a drum of water for washing since the man looked so clean.

"You must be David Arthur Bushden?" Bruton said.

"That's right. But who are you?"

"Police officers," Aveyard said. "We'd begun to think we'd never find you."

"I'm glad that you did."

"You were expecting Rupert Samuel?"

"Not really. Not any more."

"Hence the Scarlet Pimpernel?"

"I suppose my father called you in?"

"Yes, I think he'd worked it out."

"Did Rupert Samuel tell you how to get in? Ingenious, isn't it, that hydraulic pump in the hinge?"

"Ingenious. However, we have a lot to tell you. But first, I think you should come upstairs and see your mother."

CHAPTER SEVENTEEN

"You planted the bomb in the organ, didn't you?" Aveyard asked. His voice was quiet, his manner calm and conversational. David Arthur had come upstairs and both Aveyard and Bruton had stayed outside in the hall while he went in to see his mother. Neither spoke about the events in the Priests' Hole, though Porter came and expressed his surprise yet again about the way in which they had uncovered the second hiding place.

"All these years," he said, "I've lived in this house and never known. And I don't think Lord Bushden or his father can have known, either. The two little monkeys, keeping the secret all these years."

Bruton, of course, had informed Inspector Roberts that David Arthur had been found and the local and national searches had been called off. Inspector Roberts had made the appropriate entries in his book. The chief superintendent had been informed, or rather his wife had been asked to tell him when he came in from his garden. He'd want to be present when they interrogated David Arthur, though there was no doubt in Superintendent Aveyard's mind that he was responsible for the bomb. He still wasn't convinced that David Arthur had killed his brother; it didn't seem feasible, now that he had seen the young man and had spoken with him, that David Arthur could be responsible for such a crime. Of course, they'd need to add that to the interrogation; and they'd have to submit David Arthur to psychiatric tests to discover the extent of his problem.

"You did plant the bomb, didn't you?" Aveyard repeated.

"Yes."

"You wanted to kill Roger Bowman?"

"Kill him?" David Arthur said, surprised. "I wanted the organ to blow up in his face."

Aveyard stood up, walked away from David Arthur, then turned back. They were sitting in the morning room which Lady Bushden had put at Aveyard's disposal. She had wanted to be present at the interview, but he'd asked if he could conduct it with only the police there.

"Please believe me, we shall handle him very gently," he had assured her. "We certainly shan't browbeat him in any way. Apart from anything else, we have to consider that he may not be aware of what's happened." Porter, of course, had wished to draw a bath for David Arthur and had already laid out a change of clothing for him. He'd instructed to cook to prepare a light meal, "a proper meal" as he had called it. Aveyard had insisted on talking to David Arthur briefly first. Finally, both Lady Bushden and Porter had agreed.

David Arthur was sitting upright in an armchair, his hands clasped in front of him, leaning slightly forward, following what Aveyard was saying with the keen attention almost, one could have said, of a schoolboy.

"You didn't realize," Aveyard said gently, "that the organ blowing up in his face might kill him?"

"Honestly, I never even gave that a thought."

He had been cautioned, of course, before the questions began.

"Think about this, please. Think hard," Aveyard said. He glanced at Bruton who was taking notes, sitting at the table in front of the window, in a sense reinforcing the schoolroom atmosphere of which Aveyard was so conscious. "Don't answer till you have thought. Did you intend to kill Roger Bowman when you planted the bomb in the organ?" The answer to this question was vital. If David Arthur said "Yes" there would be no alternative but to charge him with attempted murder, Aveyard wanted to avoid that. He knew from what David Arthur had already said that they would charge him with Grievous Bodily Harm, but he prayed he wouldn't get a positive answer to his question.

David Arthur was thinking. At least, his brow was creased. "No," he said finally. "I didn't intend to kill him. I wanted the organ to blow up in his face."

"And you had no conception that blowing up an organ in someone's face could kill them?"

"I honestly never thought of it that way."

Both Aveyard and Bruton breathed a sigh of relief. Aveyard went to the door, called in Porter who was standing outside. "Ask Lady Bushden if she'd be so kind as to step in here," he said, "and you can draw that bath now."

David Arthur went with Porter, his step firm and springy, his face untroubled by the consequences of his action. Aveyard had sent for Dr. Samson, and had arranged for a consultant psychiatrist they sometimes used to make an appointment with Dr. Samson to see David Arthur. He had also arranged with Inspector Roberts to go to the bathroom when David Arthur undressed, and to put all his clothing into a plastic bag to take to John Victor for forensic examination.

Lady Bushden came immediately. "What did he say?" she asked.

Aveyard suggested they sit down and she arranged herself in the chair in which her son had sat. A constable had been in the room during David Arthur's questioning and Bruton was going to leave the room with him. "You stay, Sergeant Bruton, will you?" Aveyard said. Bruton came back in and sat again behind the desk. "Your son has admitted to placing the bomb in the church organ," Aveyard said gravely.

Lady Bushden sighed. "Why, why, would he do a thing like that?" she said, quite bewildered.

"Your son and Krancek, the gardener, talked together a lot. It appears one might also say there were friends."

"Krancek was very good with him always."

"Roger Bowman, it seems, stole a piece of music belonging to Krancek, and used it to compose the anthem which was broadcast by the B.B.C. Krancek was furious. He said to your son, no doubt not meaning it, 'I wish the organ would blow up in his face.' It's just the sort of thing a man might say when he was extremely angry."

"But David Arthur took it literally . . ."

"Yes. I suppose he thought he was doing Krancek a service."

She raised her hands to her face, and Aveyard could see she was near breaking point. "What did he say about the other matter . . . ?"

Aveyard knew she meant the death of Rupert Samuel. "I didn't question him about that yet," he said. "I've asked someone to come and see David Arthur for me, a psychiatrist we use a lot, a very good man. First of all, I want to be fair; I want to be absolutely certain that your son will understand the questions I shall be obliged to ask. To verify that he is fit to answer."

She looked up him. "That's very good of you, Superintendent," she said.

"You have no objections?"

"None whatsoever. What will happen if your psychiatrist says my son does understand?"

"Then we shall ask him questions to try to determine if he was responsible . . ."

"And if he was . . . ?"

"Then I'm afraid we shall charge him in the normal way."

"Poor David Arthur. It's not his fault, you know."

"I know," Aveyard said.

When the knock came on the door, Bruton went quickly to answer it. Dr. Samson had arrived. Aveyard went into the hall and spoke briefly to him, and the doctor went upstairs to see David Arthur. He had confused Aveyard for a moment by referring to Lord Bushden, until he remembered with a shock that of course David Arthur had now succeeded to the title. Apparently, Dr. Samson had arranged for the psychiatrist to come within the hour.

The chief superintendent rang, said his wife had given him the message. Aveyard explained everything he was doing, and the chief grunted an approval. "It'll be the best thing all round if the lad's judged to be unfit to plead, then he can be committed quietly somewhere and that will be that. It certainly sounds, from what you tell me about his planting the bomb, that he hasn't got all his buttons. You'll be bringing him in?"

"That depends on what the psychiatrist says . . ."

"By the way, who've you got? Kilpatrick?"

"Yes. If he says the lad isn't fit to plead, I thought I'd leave him here with a couple of constables and a sergeant until we've done all the preliminary paperwork."

The chief superintendent chuckled. "You realize you're making the same mistake everybody else has made . . ."

"What's that, Chief?"

"You're assuming he's guilty. What happens if Kilpatrick says the new Lord Bushden is quite fit to plead, and he denies having killed his brother? You don't have enough evidence against him to make a case if he denies it. And it strikes me that's well on the cards . . ."

Kilpatrick was a tall, quiet-spoken man in his late forties. He was wearing a dark green Harris tweed suit and brown boots and could have been taken for a superior type of gamekeeper. When he had said hello to Superintendent Aveyard, whom he knew quite well, he gazed about with an abstracted air. "Wonderful old places, these," he said, "so much atmosphere. Shall I be able to see Lord Bushden alone?"

"Yes, I've discussed it with his mother. She's in favour of your examination . . ."

"I'll bet she is," he said, "and I know what she wants me to find."

"He has a suite of rooms of his own. I thought you might like to talk with him there. Familiar surroundings and all that."

"It would be better."

"Dr. Samson's with him now, but I imagine you can go up."

Aveyard showed Kilpatrick to David Bushden's suite, next to his brother's on the first-floor landing. The contrast between the two sets of rooms could not have been greater. David Arthur's rooms were littered with the clutter of an active life. The sitting room was practically a workshop, with meccano, modelling kits, and a Leggo town. There were hundreds of books in the bookcases, many of the "Practical Carpentry" type. In one corner of the room was an electronic equipment set and something had been built from the various transistors and wires and dials it contained. There was a degutted radio, and even the gearbox of a car that had been taken apart, its gear wheels showing in the housing like the viscera of some future robot. All across one wall were tools mounted on clips, and Aveyard felt a pang of envy. He'd always promised himself that as soon as he could afford it, he'd turn the spare room of his flat into a workshop. David Arthur had literally every tool that could be required for any task he cared to undertake. Aveyard marvelled at the neatness of the display, the precise order of the spanners, chisels, screwdrivers and pliers.

He could see Kilpatrick glance round in the seconds before Samson greeted him, no doubt drawing a dozen conclusions from what he could immediately see. Samson said hello gravely, but the two men didn't shake hands. However, when Samson introduced Kilpatrick to Lord Bushden, Kilpatrick stuck out his hand and Lord Bushden took it and shook it vigorously with no trace of shyness or nervousness, though Aveyard knew Samson had explained the reason for Kilpatrick's visit.

Samson caught Aveyard's eye. "I think we could go

below," he said, and Aveyard nodded, casting a last envious glance at the tools as they went out together.

"You explained to Mr. Kilpatrick that this is only a preliminary examination?" Aveyard said as they were walking downstairs.

"Yes. It shouldn't take long. I said you merely wanted to know at this juncture if Lord Bushden was fit to answer questions. Medically he's quite sound; the stay in the Priests' Hole has done him no damage at all so far as I can tell. He always was a healthy active young man."

"Unlike his brother?"

Dr. Samson looked at him, debating whether he could discuss the health of a patient now that the patient were dead. "Yes, I suppose you could say that. Unlike his brother." He thought for a few moments as they stood in the hall. "I suppose Mr. Kilpatrick could tell you much more about this, and normally I don't like being an amateur psychologist, but seeing patients all the time, as I do, you get to understand a little about them. Rupert Samuel was the typical second son. Second sons, I suppose, are a special breed. They either go completely into themselves, since they know they cannot compete with the heir, can never hope to have the same consideration as the heir, or they become fiercely aggressive, determined to make up in achievement what they lack in birth. 'I'll show him,' they say, 'that I can be as good as him.' That's what happened to Rupert Samuel. He always had this enormous drive to achieve something. That's why he was so brilliant in all his studies; he had to be brilliant to 'show them.'

"But of course, that left him with a grave deficiency in other respects. He wasn't easy to talk to because his mind was so crystal clear and people don't tend to be lucid in their everyday speech and lives. He couldn't tolerate other peoples mediocrity, and that showed. Poor chap. He knew how unpopular he was, and he wanted so desperately to be liked. Many times he used to say to me, 'my greatest problem is to

make people understand how false most emotion can be!' He
saw the enormous expenditure, for example, of time and
effort and money that Lord Bushden—his father, I mean,
not his brother—put into the ordinary lives of the village
people, and he said they should be made to be totally in-
dependent. He intended, for example, but only after his father had died, to sell the houses to the occupants. He said
that people should be made to realize the value of capital,
should be taught to care, to save up to buy something solid
on a mortgage. You know, in many ways he was right. People *should* learn to stand on their own feet. Most of the cot-
tages in the village are let at totally uneconomic rents. One
part of the estate subsidizes another. To repair one house
alone mops up anything the estate might get from renting
that house for as many as five or ten years. Rupert Samuel
wanted to make each part of the estate self-sufficient. Selling
the houses to the tenants would have helped both the tenants and the estate. But, of course, it was a difficult problem.
How do you persuade people to understand it could be better to pay five pounds a week to repay a mortgage, than one
pound a week for rent? In his anxiety, he used to over-eat.
He was a compulsive eater. He didn't want anyone to know
about it and kept food in his room . . ."

"I've seen it," Aveyard said. "Frankfurters and potato
salad . . ."

"The wrong things, of course, for a man who took virtually no exercise. But he'd almost become paranoid about
going into the village and the farms to chat to the tenants.
Of course, since they never saw him just to pass the time of
day and only when he had a clipboard in his hand telling
them what they were doing wrong, the tenants got quite a
bad impression of him. Which he knew, and which only
made things worse for him. Poor chap. I felt really sorry for
him."

"And David Arthur . . . ?"

"Well, that's a tragedy. He, of course, has the gift of getting on with people. Everybody likes him. He's open, un-complicated, simple . . ."

"Hardly uncomplicated . . ."

"I meant purely in the social sense. The villagers all loved him. He used to stop and chat with them, you see. He was interested in everything. You've seen his tools. Anybody in the village who had anything tricky they wanted fixed used to come to him. Anything. And he'd work it out." He gave an embarrassed cough. "Actually, he helped me once. I had a large fridge and the thermostat packed up. It was old but it had served me well and fitted into a space in my kitchen. I couldn't get the thermostat replaced, and no one could be bothered to repair it, so I asked David Arthur about it one day. Do you know, he came to my house, took out the ther-mostat, brought it here, and fixed it. It's never given me a moment's trouble since then. He showed it to me in bits, tried to explain it to me, but I'm afraid I'm no good at that sort of thing. He even bought a book on automatic controls, and had read it, just so he could do that little job for me."

"And this is the man the psychiatrist is examining at this moment to discover if he is fit to answer questions . . . ?"

"The human mind is a wonderful yet a terrible organism, Superintendent. We know so little about it. We're groping in the dark, it sometimes seems to me."

"It all points to schizophrenia, doesn't it? One part of him brilliant with his hands, a good craftsman, the other part of him, what you might call the conventional morality part of him, an absolute simpleton. I'm convinced he didn't even stop to think of the consequences of planting that explosive in the church organ. I'm convinced he took Krancek's words quite literally . . ."

Dr. Samson nodded gravely. Mr. Kilpatrick was coming down the stairs. Aveyard led the way into the dining room and they sat in a group of armchairs at the far end, out of earshot of the constables, Inspector Roberts and Sergeant Bruton.

"You understand this was only a brief preliminary interview," Kilpatrick said, "but that's what I was told you wanted. The answer to one question. Is Lord Bushden fit to answer questions? In other words, is he capable of understanding the question, formulating a reply, and understanding his own reply."

"That's right," Aveyard said. "What is your opinion?"

"Without a doubt, Lord Bushden is capable of understanding any question you might put to him. He's capable of logical thought about that question, and of giving you a coherent reply based on those thoughts."

"Does he know right from wrong?" Aveyard asked, but Kilpatrick held up his hands.

"You mustn't ask me anything else," he said. "Specifically, I didn't go into questions of moral responsibility at this stage. Right and wrong are such complex matters, Superintendent. At a later stage we shall have to ask ourselves, does he know the boundaries of conventional morality, does he understand about the framework of our laws, can he distinguish between what the majority of people call right and wrong. But I was not asked to begin an examination along those lines, and I have not done so. That's a far more lengthy process. Then there is the question of schizophrenia, which has been mentioned, or in fact any other mental illness. These are all things I will go into at a later stage, if I am asked to do so. For the moment all I can say is, yes, you may ask him your questions, confident he will know what you are saying, that if he answers those questions his answers will be based on a system of his own experience and progressive logical thought."

"That will do for me," Aveyard said. He went down the dining room and asked Inspector Roberts to get him a call to the chief superintendent. "He'll be at home," Aveyard said, "most probably in the house having a cup of tea at this time of day."

Dr. Samson and Mr. Kilpatrick said goodbye as they went

out, discussing Lord Bushden in medical terms incompre-
hensible to any layman. Aveyard knew all that would come
later, the lego-medical battle in the courtroom, with the
psychiatrist the defence would brief doing his best to prove
some species of insanity. "Let's pray it doesn't come into
court," Aveyard said to Bruton. "Kilpatrick says he's fit to
answer questions and it'll be one of those cases barristers
love to get their high-priced teeth into. I'd rather see him
put quietly away."

Bruton looked at him, and Aveyard could see he was
slightly shocked, even surprised by the words. "You're
usually dead hot on a vigorous prosecution," Bruton said,
but then he had to correct himself. "Come to think of it, it's
only criminals you really go for strongly. You tend to look
for ways out for these—what I might call amateurs . . ."

"I wouldn't call the man who wielded that sword an amateur—in the sense you mean the word. It seems to me he
swung it with an almost professional skill."

They took David Arthur to the Police Headquarters in
Birton. All the brass was there—the chief constable, the
assistant chief constable, the chief superintendent, an inspector from the legal department, a superintendent from
the prosecutor's office, and the senior partner of the Bushden
family lawyers, Ormorod and Peabody, Jimmy Ormorod
himself. Ormorod and the chief constable had been in consultation with the superintendent from the prosecutor's
office; a Peer of the Realm has certain rights and privileges
when it comes to legal action being taken against him, and
Ormorod had been at pains to point out exactly what these
were. He had agreed to permit a preliminary questioning of
his client, but had reserved the right to stop the interrogation at any time. There had also been much discussion about
who should conduct the interrogation, but the chief superintendent had said he felt strongly that it should be Superintendent Aveyard. Ormorod had raised no objection to that,
subject of course to his client's approval. When Lord Bush-

den arrived, Ormorod and he were permitted to be alone together in the chief constable's sitting room. Jimmy advised David Arthur of his rights. David Arthur listened. He surprised Jimmy by knowing exactly what those rights were. "It's something my father taught me," he explained.

"There's just one thing, Lord Bushden . . ."

"Oh, call me David Arthur, Mr. Ormorod, as you always have done . . ."

"Very well, David Arthur. I must speak to you very frankly. In British law, no man is ever asked questions until it has been ascertained that he's mentally equipped to answer them. Do you know what I mean?"

"Yes, the psychiatrist's examination. Mr. Kilpatrick. I thought him a very agreeable man."

"Good. Mr. Kilpatrick maintains that you are fit to answer any questions they may put to you . . ."

"I should jolly well hope so . . ."

"Hold on a minute. If you wish, I can ask them to adjourn the proceedings today until we've had a chance to consult a psychiatrist of our own. I was thinking of Mr. Hepplewhite who knows you so well . . ."

"I can't stand him . . ."

"I know you can't. You've told me so often in the past. But perhaps he might not agree to the verdict of Mr. Kilpatrick. He might think you're *not* fit to answer questions . . ."

"Oh, I don't want that. I want to answer the questions. I think it might be rather interesting."

Jimmy Ormorod's face was grave. "Rather interesting, David Arthur? In what way?"

"It's something I've never experienced before. It would be interesting to see how they go about it."

"David Arthur, it's my duty to remind you you're not here to be 'interested.' You're here to be interrogated, about matters of a serious nature. As a result of that interrogation, you could be charged with a capital offence, for which the penalty could be a long term of confinement. Do you quite clearly understand that . . . ?"

"Oh yes, I get all that. It's up to them to ask me questions to try to get to the truth of the matter. If the truth of the matter is that I have done something wrong, I'll have to pay for it, and the payment won't be money, it'll be imprisonment."

Jimmy Ormorod had deliberately not used the word imprisonment. He knew he could get David Arthur sentenced to a mental institution, if that seemed the better course when all the evidence had been heard. But he was gravely troubled by his client's attitude. The only thing he wanted to ask, but dare not, was, "Did you kill your brother? Did you try to kill Roger Bowman?" He knew David Arthur's mother had told him about the two deaths, but she had not gone into many details, and surprisingly he had not asked for any. On the telephone Lady Bushden told him David Arthur had accepted both pieces of news with very little sign of emotion. He'd nodded when she told him about his father, but then, they had all been expecting the death. But when she told him about Rupert Samuel being killed with a sword, he had merely said, "Oh dear." And so far as he was concerned, that subject was closed. Several minutes later, after thought, he had said, "I suppose that means I shall have to run the estate." She had not answered that question.

They went back into the conference room. The police were sitting round the large centre table and rose as a man when Lord Bushden entered. Superintendent Aveyard was sitting half-way along the table; a chair had been placed for Lord Bushden across from Aveyard's position. Ormorod was sitting beside him on his right. The chief constable was on Aveyard's right, the chief superintendent on his left. The stenographer borrowed from the County Court was sitting to the left of Lord Bushden. Ormorod began the proceedings by identifying each officer at the table, all of whom he knew either professionally or from the two social clubs in Birton. As

he introduced each officer and explained his function, Lord
Bushden said, "How do you do," in a clear voice. Each
police officer said, "How do you do" back, all somewhat con-
strained. When Ormorod came to Superintendent Aveyard,
David Arthur said, "We've met, but hello."

Superintendent Aveyard said hello back. Then he began
the proceedings. "We're gathered here today to conduct an
investigation into the events of Bushden Hall and the village
of Bushden during the past few days. This is an informal
meeting and the notes that are being taken are for our own
information. The matter of their possible further use will be
the subject of a separate discussion between Mr. Ormorod
and the chief constable. Let me begin by listing these
events. Firstly, the decease of Lord Bushden, a matter which
would not have required police intervention had Lord Bushden himself, shortly before his death, not asked a police
officer to be brought to him. Secondly, the death of Rupert
Samuel Bushden, in circumstances which indicate the possible commission of a crime."

Aveyard paused for a moment, his eyes never leaving the
face of David Arthur. Aveyard knew he'd been told about
his brother's death, but had no idea what his reaction might
be, faced with the knowledge again in such awesome surroundings. He'd have preferred to conduct this investigation
alone with David Arthur, or possibly with Ormorod present
and the chief inspector, but he could see the issues of title
had to be covered, as well as the matter of possible insanity.
He had no doubt that David Arthur must be feeling as awed
as Aveyard himself did. Though he showed no signs of it. He
was leaning slightly forward in his chair, looking from one to
the other, but giving all his attention to Aveyard when he
spoke, as if Aveyard were a magician about to pull a rabbit
from a hat.

"However, " Aveyard continued, "I would prefer to deal
with the third matter first, if that is acceptable to everybody.
The explosion of the church organ."

He looked at Ormorod when he spoke the last words. He had already told Ormorod on the telephone that David Arthur had confessed to planting the bomb. He had also said that during his questioning David Arthur had stated he had no intention of causing the death of the vicar, the victim of the bomb, nor of Roger Bowman for whom the bomb was intended. Both of them knew perfectly well that under the law, anyone who commits an offence which results in the death of or injury to a third party has no defence by saying he didn't intend it for that party. For the purposes of the law, it was irrelevant who was sitting at the organ at the time the bomb exploded.

"I understand that certain questions have already been put to Lord Bushden concerning this matter," Ormorod said, "and provided it can be demonstrated in the proper place that everything was done in a correct manner, as to cautioning, etc., I have no objection to those questions being repeated."

Lord Bushden nodded his head. "No objection at all," he said.

"Lord Bushden, you have already been cautioned according to the regulations at present in force. At approximately nine fifty-five hours this morning, an explosive device went off in the organ of the church in Bushden. Injury was caused to the vicar, who was playing the organ at the time. A subsequent investigation revealed that a bomb had been planted within the organ in such a manner that it would explode a few minutes after the organ was switched on. I must now ask you the following question: are you the person who placed that explosive device inside the organ?"

"Yes, I am," David Arthur said, without looking at Ormorod.

"Are you the person responsible for the manufacture of that explosive device?"

"Yes, I am."

"Are you the person responsible for the design and construction of the arming device which caused the explosion to take place?"

"Yes," David Arthur said, "I am."

"Do you accept, therefore, that you are the person responsible for the subsequent explosion of that device, and therefore the injuries to the vicar of Bushden, the Reverend Thomas Dalgleish, aged fifty, of the Old Vicarage, Bushden?"

"Yes, I see that," David Arthur said.

Ormorod looked at Aveyard, looked at Lord Bushden.

Several of the police officers were looking at Aveyard and the inspector from the legal department leaned forward as if to catch Aveyard's attention. But Aveyard was already speaking. "It's not enough to "see" it, Lord Bushden," he said. "Do you *accept* that you are the person responsible for the subsequent explosion of that device and therefore the injuries caused to the vicar of Bushden, the Reverend Thomas Dalgleish, aged fifty, of the Old Vicarage, Bushden?"

"Yes," David Arthur said quietly. "I do accept that. Look, may I say something?" He hurried on without giving Ormorod a chance to stop him. "Look, I'm really sorry it happened to Tom Dalgleish. I mean, he was a good chap, really, and I didn't mean him any harm . . ."

"Stop there," Ormorod said. "Please, David Arthur, stop there." He turned to the table at large. "You understand, gentlemen, that even though my client has just said he meant the vicar no harm, there is no implication of intention in his words that he meant the other chap, Roger Bowman, any harm. I understand the question of malice will be very important to this particular charge, and I would not like that question to be influenced, or prejudged, by my client's natural expression of sympathy for the vicar."

Aveyard looked down the table at the inspector from the legal department. He was grinning, but nodded his head. Aveyard was pleased the matter had been raised and dealt with; he didn't want to run aground on a purely legal technicality. As ever, he was concerned that justice should be done. It was obvious to them all that Lord Bushden had planted the bomb; whether he had done so "with malice aforethought" was a matter for a judge and jury, which might well turn out to be a panel of Lords and Ladies, Lord Bushden's "peers."

Aveyard turned and spoke to the chief superintendent. Though his voice was low, he knew that all present could hear what he was saying. "I'd like to leave the matter of the explosive device now, Chief Superintendent?"

The chief superintendent nodded his assent without referring the matter to anybody else. He felt, no doubt as Aveyard did, that matters of motive were better left undealt with at this moment.

"Turning now to the second incident. The death of Rupert Samuel. Can you, Lord Bushden, give us an account of your movements on the afternoon of Friday?"

David Arthur looked at Ormorod for assent. Ormorod nodded, but added, "Just the facts, no opinions, no apologies."

David Arthur thought for a while. "I suppose what you're after," he said, "is an account of how I came to be in the Priests' Hole?"

Aveyard nodded.

"Well, I shall have to give you a bit of the prehistory. Rupert Samuel had talked to me a lot about when Father died. He'd said what they would do to me when Father died, that they wouldn't let me inherit the title; they'd put me away and that would be that. I didn't want the title necessarily, but I didn't want to be put away. So I agreed when Rupert Samuel suggested a scheme. He said I should write Father a note to suggest I'd done away with myself. Then, when Father died, they couldn't put me away inside an asylum. After the funeral, he said he would gather a crowd of people in the house, and I could come back again out of hiding. The idea was that I should stay down in the Priests' Hole until after the funeral."

Ormorod interrupted him. "Any questions so far, Super-intendent?"

Aveyard said, "I prefer to let Lord Bushden finish first."

"But have you any questions on the part so far?"

"How can I tell you, Mr. Ormorod? It may well be that some question may arise out of something as yet unsaid which relates to what we've already heard. But as I just said, I prefer to let Lord Bushden *finish* first . . ."

Ormorod took the reproof with a faint smile. He had achieved his objective of giving Lord Bushden time to think.

"So, on Friday afternoon, Mother told us at lunch that she'd been speaking with the doctor and he had said that Father didn't have long to last. We both went up, sepa-rately, and saw Father. As it turned out, it was the last time for me, though I don't know about Rupert Samuel so I can't speak for him." He looked sideways at Ormorod, then back at Aveyard. "I'm trying to stick to what I know, you see," he said, "and I don't know about Rupert Samuel's movements after he left me in the Priests' Hole. Come to think of it, I haven't told you how we got there, have I? Well, after we'd both seen Father, Rupert Samuel came to my room. He said that I had to go into the Priests' Hole at once, and I should write the note. I'd begun to have a few doubts but decided to go along with him and so I wrote the note. When he came to my room, I was actually pressing some flowers to go into a nature study book I'm making, and as a bit of a joke I decided to put the flower I was pressing into the envelope."

Again it's there, Aveyard thought, this streak in David Ar-thur. During the serious moments a frivolous note comes into his actions. A lack of comprehension, perhaps of the consequences of his actions. Like the bomb in the organ; do something and don't ask what will happen as a result.

"We went together down into the Priests' Hole. The sec-ond one, where you found me. Rupert Samuel had already put food in there for me and candles. I knew I'd be all right. When we were young, we used to sneak out of bed and spend nights down there, so I wasn't afraid. But when Rupert Samuel went out, he bolted the door, and that worried me because it wasn't part of the arrangement. We'd never discussed bolting me in. I panicked a little, but I knew there was nothing to be done so I sat and waited till he came back. Then you came in with your sergeant and took me upstairs again, and Mother told me Rupert Samuel had been killed with a sword, so he couldn't have come back for me, could he?"

He was silent, the question hanging in the air. Aveyard shifted on his seat. "No, I suppose he couldn't," he said. "I have just a couple of small questions. First, what did you mean when you said in your note, I go to join those Lords and Ladies we have so often admired together?"

"That was a private thing between Father and me. He always said that in matters of principle one should be quite constant and inflexible. He didn't think any man should hold public office who had sinned, however small the sin might be. I remember he was very much in support of the Oscar Wilde play, about a chap who resigns from the Government. The ones in particular he admired were people who, in the last extreme, were willing to give their lives for something in which they believed. It was my way of suggesting I'd gone to kill myself rather than inherit the title."

"You believed your father would understand what you meant?"

"I'm sorry, there's something I haven't explained. You see, Rupert Samuel wasn't going to give that note to my father. He was going to wait until after my father was dead, and then hide it somewhere in Father's room where it would be found."

"May I ask why you didn't write something more explicit, something like, Dear Father, I do not want the title and would rather kill myself . . . ?"

"Oh, I had quite a difficulty with Rupert Samuel over that," he said. "He wanted me to do what you suggested, in almost exactly those words, but I couldn't, you see. I couldn't bring myself to tell a direct lie. That's why I said what I did about joining those Lords and Ladies we admired so much, you know, people who went to the Tower rather than sacrifice a principle, that sort of thing."

Aveyard was silent now, reviewing in his mind what Lord Bushden had said. It all made sense, of course, provided one could accept the nature of the two brothers, the characters of each of them. It now was apparent to Aveyard that, if what David Arthur had said was true, his brother meant to murder him. Meant to leave him to rot in that second Priests' Hole. Quite obviously, Rupert Samuel could not bring himself to kill his brother by a positive act such as a bullet from a gun, a blow from a sword . . . But could the same be said of David Arthur? He was the man for direct action, even if his principles did cause him to write such a bizarre letter.

"Am I correct in saying the last time you saw your brother was when he went out of the second Priests' Hole, the room in which I found you after I had unbolted the door?"

"Yes, that's right."

"Did you strike your brother a blow with a sword . . . ?"

"I think I must object to that, Superintendent," Ormorod said. "Lord Bushden has stated quite clearly the last time he saw his brother; any matter concerning the manner of Mr. Rupert Samuel's death can only cause my client grave and unnecessary distress."

"I don't mind answering the question," David Arthur said. "No, I didn't hit him with a sword. I didn't see him again after he locked me in." Ormorod was shaking his head looking at David Arthur, marvelling no doubt at his lack of sorrow, his complete lack of emotion.

Aveyard turned to the chief superintendent again. "I'd be prepared to end matters at that," he said. "The Legal Department and the Prosecutor's Office can take over from here."

"There is just one question I'd like to ask," the chief superintendent said, "as a matter of record. If you don't mind?"

"I don't mind," Aveyard said.

"Lord Bushden, you said if I remember correctly that you placed a piece of a plant into the envelope of the letter you had written to your father. Was the fact of the plant being a Scarlet Pimpernel of any special significance? Or was it just that it happened to be the plant most handy at the time . . . ?"

"I don't quite understand what you mean by special significance. My father and I were both greatly interested in plants, you know. We often used to put something in the envelope when we sent a note to each other."

"One final question, Lord Bushden. Have you ever read any of the works of Baroness Orczy?"

"Chief Superintendent, I really must object . . ." Ormorod said. Everyone was looking at the chief superintendent in surprise. But he smiled benignly at Lord Bushden, unmoved by the confusion he was causing.

"No, I can't say I have," David Bushden said. "What field does it come in, politics, history . . . ?"

"No, I'm afraid they are works of historical fiction," the chief superintendent said, "and I don't suppose you read much fiction?"

"No, I'm afraid I don't," Lord Bushden said.

The meeting was adjourned; Lord Bushden was sent back to Bushden Hall under police escort, Jimmy Ormorod went into another meeting with the officers from the Legal Department and the Prosecutor's Office; the chief constable and the assistant chief constable held a meeting with the chief superintendent, and Aveyard went back to his flat. He had radioed from his car, and Jim Bruton was waiting when he arrived. He opened the door of the flat and they went in together. "You didn't mind coming here, Jim?" he said. "I wanted to get away from people for a while."

"I don't know whether to take that as an insult or a compliment," Jim Bruton said, but he understood very well. He'd had these sessions with the brass at Police Headquarters; they could be very trying. "There's nothing of note in the Incidents Book," he said.

Aveyard was in the kitchen, making coffee. "That smells good," Bruton said. He was prowling around the sitting room, looking at nothing in particular. Aveyard came through with the coffee, and they sat down.

"It was as we thought it would be," he said. "He told us how and why Rupert Samuel had locked him in the second Priests' Hole."

"And was it also as we thought that Rupert Samuel was trying to get rid of him, but couldn't bring himself to do the job?"

"We'll never know for sure, but that's what I think."

"I do too."

They both fell silent, both no doubt thinking of the horror of the situation, the terrible hatred that would cause a man to lock up his own brother, and sentence him to a slow lingering death. Better that he had put a shotgun to his ear, or had hit him with a sword.

"You checked the Priests' Hole?" asked Aveyard.

"Yes, and I could find no way that David Arthur could have got in or out. At one time there was an exit, but I checked the plans again and when the extension was built for the boiler room for the central heating, the engineers must have built over it, without realizing a concealed door was there. I found a small grating in the floor, and another one high up so you can get a flow of air in the room; a chemical toilet was behind that curtain as you had supposed, and beyond that a small alcove. At the end of the alcove was a solid stone wall; at least it looked solid, but I fished round a bit and found another of those hinge mechanisms. This time, it was an iron sconce on the wall. Turn it and pull down, and the door pivots at the middle. It gave me the creeps, I can tell you. On the other side, I was staring straight at a new wall built of those insulating blocks, the inner skin of the new boiler house. I went and checked."

"It was absolutely impossible for David Arthur to get in and out again?"

"I even checked the door with the three bolts we found fastened, to see if it could be lifted off its hinges. It couldn't. It all gave me the creeps, I can tell you."

"You said that before . . . It still doesn't help us to know who killed Rupert Samuel."

The telephone rang and Aveyard picked it up. He gave the number. It was the chief superintendent.

"You did very well this afternoon, Bill," he said, "but why didn't you ask about the death of Lord Bushden? David Arthur might have known why he sent for the police."

"I wanted to keep that one in reserve, Chief," Bill Aveyard said.

The chief superintendent chuckled. "You haven't finished with David Arthur then?"

"Oh yes, I've finished with him. He didn't murder his brother, I'm convinced of that."

"Then who did?"

"I only have one suspect."

"When are you going to arrest him?"

"I'm not. He's dead."

"Rupert Samuel? You think he did it himself?"

Now it was Aveyard's turn to chuckle. "You're making the same mistake we've all been making," he said. "The reason why Lord Bushden wanted to see a policeman, the reason he wouldn't tell his wife, or his vicar or his butler, was because he'd just killed his own son. And didn't want to die with it on his conscience."

Jim Bruton was looking at him, and nodding. He'd come to the same conclusion.

"Can you prove it, Bill?"

"I'm going to have a damn good try."

He put the phone down. Then he picked it up again and took it off its cradle. "Now we won't be interrupted," he said. "This is the way I see it . . ." Jim Bruton settled back.

"Imagine the scene. Rupert Samuel has locked his brother in the second Priests' Hole. We have to think about the special conditions of the Bushden title. If David Arthur were alive at the death of his father, he would inherit the title. If he were to marry and have a son, that son would get the title in his turn. But if David Arthur were alive when his father died, and he inherited the title, then he subsequently died before producing an heir, that title could not be passed out of the direct line of succession, that is to say, Rupert Samuel couldn't inherit it. Therefore, David Arthur had to die first. Hence the suicide note. But of course, Rupert Samuel wouldn't sit on the suicide note, would he, because if there was any question that David Arthur had not died before his father, there could be doubt about the title and the succession. Therefore, it's my guess that Rupert Samuel, having bolted his brother in the second Priests' Hole, immediately came upstairs and showed his father the note. "Look," he said, "David Arthur *has* killed himself." His father, don't forget, was lying on his death bed and wouldn't go rushing about the place. He'd depend on Rupert Samuel to do things for him. He'd lie in bed and wait, expecting at any moment that Lady Bushden would come upstairs and share with him the terrible news of their son's death. We know how close they were. We know they shared the same bedroom, the same upstairs sitting room, played word games together. She said, 'Quite simply, he was my whole life.' So here is Lord Bushden, lying on his death bed waiting for something to happen that doesn't. Meanwhile, he's thinking. Of course, he re-reads the bit about Lords and Ladies, thinks of the Ice Tower. But the plant in the envelope isn't a Lords and Ladies. He knows Lords and Ladies is out of season anyway. Suddenly, he realizes that Rupert Samuel is the key to all this, and even begins to think perhaps Rupert Samuel is more involved than he should be. All right so far?"

"I'm following you," Jim Bruton said.

"Lord Bushden works out, wrongly as it turns out, that the Scarlet Pimpernel was included to warn him Rupert Samuel is up to no good. We know what Lord Bushden thought about Rupert Samuel and the way he was handling the village which meant so much to Lord Bushden. He summons all his energy, goes along the corridor in a fit of blinding anger, thinking about Rupert Samuel . . ."

"But first puts on his dressing gown . . ."

"That's right, Jim, puts on his dressing gown, goes along the corridor and grabs the first thing that comes to hand, a large double-edged sword. He opens the door of Rupert Samuel's room, finds him with his back to the door, crosses the carpet, and whack! brings the sword down on Rupert Samuel's neck. He drops the sword, goes back to his own room, and calls for the police."

"Don't forget he also sees some of the Scarlet Pimpernel on Rupert Samuel's floor . . ."

"Since, of course, Rupert Samuel had either opened the letter, or it hadn't been sealed by David Arthur. Maybe Rupert Samuel took out the letter, dropped a bit of the Scarlet Pimpernel on the floor without noticing it."

Aveyard sat back. Bruton sat back.

"It all sounds feasible," Jim Bruton said.

Aveyard poured them both another cup of coffee, his face gloomy. "Yes, Jim, but how the hell are we going to prove it?"

"No footprints on the carpet because of the vacuum cleaner."

"No fingerprints on the handle of the sword."

"Nothing."

"So, we've had all that sweat for nothing . . . ?"

Silence again, a deep thinking silence. Suddenly Aveyard sat up.

"Sweat? It might just be, it might just be." He put the telephone back on the hook, waited a second and took it off again. He had to do it a couple of times before he got the dialling tone. Then he dialled a number.

"Is that John?" he asked, "John Victor?" It obviously was. "You may think I'm crazy, but could you tell me if it's worth while doing two things. Firstly, washing the handle of that sword, the green velvet, and then washing Lord Bushden's hands, and comparing the two? It might be? Good, well, I'll be right down. Would you like to make a start."

He got out of the chair. "When you mentioned sweat, it occurred to me," he said as he and Bruton were putting on their coats, "that if Lord Bushden was angry, and ill, perhaps he sweated. And if he sweated, that green velvet would pick it up, and John Victor might be able to isolate it. It seems to be worth a try."

They drove together in Bruton's car to the police laboratory. When they arrived, John Victor showed them two test-tubes. Both contained a milky liquid.

"One's from the sword, the other's from Lord Bushden. We might be even luckier than we had a right to hope," he said. "I've had a word with Dr. Samson. He was treating Lord Bushden with a medicine to keep down the pain and help him to sleep, an analgesic. If you want the chemical name, it's magnesium dimethyl-oxyquinazine-methylene-methyl-amino-sulphonate. We're in luck, because that chemical would show up in Lord Bushden's sweat glands, in small amounts of course, but the test for magnesium is extremely sensitive, and so is the oxyquinazine test. In either case, we can detect one part in a million. I've already found they both contain magnesium."

On the desk in front of him was a comparison spectrophotometer. Light passing through a prism could be made to illuminate either of the two test-tubes, now mounted in stainless steel clips. Above the machine was a large dial. John Victor turned a switch, and the light shone through the first test-tube. He took a pipette and used it to suck up a tiny quantity of liquid from a bottle of re-agent. He watched the pipette carefully while permitting some of the liquid to escape. When he had the exact amount, as measured by a ground glass line on the neck of the pipette, he added the liquid to the contents of the test-tube. He unclipped the test-tube and shook it gently. The contents slowly turned a delicate lime green. He put the test-tube back in its clip. Then he took the second test-tube and repeated the process. That too turned a delicate lime green and he clipped that back, next to the first one.

"Does the fact that they've both turned green tell you anything?" Aveyard asked, impatient.

"Only that both contain the quinazine group," John Victor said, "but many drugs do."

He turned the switch at the bottom and the centre of the machine. The needle on the dial at the top of the machine slowly crept up. When it had reached a reading of 7.45 it stopped.

"Now we shall find out," he said. He moved the switch that diverted the light from one test-tube to the other, turned the bottom switch again. Aveyard and Bruton watched, completely absorbed, as the needle slowly rose. When it reached six both had stopped breathing. When it got to seven they could hardly contain themselves. The needle finally stopped on 7.45.

"Lord Bushden handled that sword," Aveyard said.

John Victor shook his head. "You'll never prove that," he said. "All that test tells us is that someone handled that sword whose hand had sweated and who had ingested a quantity of a medicine containing magnesium dimethyl-oxyquinazine-methylene-methylamino-sulphonate."

"And that could be Lord Bushden?"

"Yes, but it could also be a lot of other people."

CHAPTER EIGHTEEN

Sunday night in the village, and Superintendent Aveyard walked along the driveway of Bushden Hall beneath the trees, seeing the light in the first-floor window which streamed out over the grounds. He'd met Dr. Samson at the entrance. "Just popping in to see Lady Bushden," Samson had said as they walked up the drive together. Both had parked their cars outside the large entrance gates which were never closed.

"I'm glad David Arthur is going into a hospital. We shall be able to look after him properly," he said.

"He is schizophrenic?"

"I think you could say that. I've thought it all along, but it's been very difficult to treat him in the past as he should have been treated. Oddly enough, Lord Bushden agreed with me, but Lady Bushden was set against it. I suppose we shall never know how much mental sickness is caused by the influence of family, how much by hereditary defects, how much by actual physical damage, often during the act of birth itself. I know we could have helped more if we had had the control the boy needed. On the one hand a benign father, teaching him everything he could; on the other hand a mother saying, as she did for many years, there's nothing wrong with my boy; and then a vicious and malicious brother."

"Also an indulgent butler?"

"I suppose one must also include Porter."

Amanda Tew came out of the house as they arrived. "Did you want to see Lady Bushden?" Dr. Samson said. "If so, do you mind awfully if I go first? I have to be at a confinement later . . ."

"No, I wasn't going in," Aveyard said.

The doctor rang the bell, and Porter came to the door.

Aveyard had stood waiting at the bottom step while Amanda Tew came down. She was wearing a coat and a dress, stockings and smart shoes. "I was surprised when you telephoned," she said, as she linked her arm in his. "Where are you taking me?"

"Anywhere," he said, "so long as there are no Lords and Ladies."

They set off together down the drive. As they passed through the gate they saw Jim Beddle shuffling along, his old dog beside him. They watched as the dog cocked his leg against the pillarbox.

"There, tha' can do it when tha' tries," Jim Beddle said, and touched his forelock as the car swept by.